'This house is

'It's you who are m

'Roberts. The name ~~~~ Roberts, not lady, not sweetheart, and not any of the other names you keep on calling me!'

'I don't give a damn what your name is!' Nick said. 'Let's get this straight. I am going for a swim now and when I get back I don't want to find any sign of you here!'

Dear Reader

Wouldn't it be wonderful to drop everything and jet off to Australia—the land of surf, sunshine, 'barbies' and, of course, the vast, untamed Outback? Mills & Boon contemporary romances offer you that very chance! Tender and exciting love stories by favourite Australian authors bring vividly to life the city, beach and bush, and introduce you to the most gorgeous heroes that Down Under has to offer…check out your local shops, or with our Readers' Service, for a trip of a lifetime!

The Editor

Jennifer Taylor was born in Liverpool, England, and still lives in the North-West, several miles outside the city. Books have always been a passion of hers, so it seemed natural to choose a career in librarianship, a wise decision as the library was where she met her husband, Bill. Twenty years and two children later, they are still happily married, she is still working in the library, with the added bonus that she has discovered how challenging and enjoyable writing romantic fiction can be!

Recent titles by the same author:

GUILTY OF LOVE

LOVE IS
A RISK

BY
JENNIFER TAYLOR

MILLS & BOON LIMITED
ETON HOUSE   18-24 PARADISE ROAD
RICHMOND   SURREY   TW9 1SR

*First published in Great Britain 1992
by Mills & Boon Limited*

© Jennifer Taylor 1992

*Australian copyright 1992
Philippine copyright 1992
This edition 1992*

ISBN 0 263 77576 3

*Set in Times Roman 11 on 12 pt.
01-9206-47840 C*

Made and printed in Great Britain

CHAPTER ONE

SUN, sea and sand—that was what the brochure had promised, even in October, and that was what she'd been expecting, not this gale-force wind and driving rain which made Heraklion airport look like a wasteland!

With a weary sigh, Neeve turned away from the window and looked round the near-deserted waiting-room. For nearly three hours now she'd been waiting for the taxi to arrive to take her to the villa she'd rented, but there was still no sign of its arrival. The other passengers who had flown to Crete with her had left the airport ages back and were now probably comfortably installed in their hotels.

She was the only one who had booked to go to the less popular southernly coast of the island to a tiny village some miles from the town of Ierápetra, although at this rate it was doubtful if she'd get there before her two weeks were up! Still, she should have expected something else would go wrong to add to all the other mishaps. If she'd been less stubborn, then she would have accepted what fate had been trying to tell her three weeks back and cancelled the whole ill-fated trip. But no, she had pig-headedly decided to go on, so she only had herself to blame. After all, how many jilted brides insisted on going on the honeymoon . . . alone?

'Miss Roberts? Miss Nia . . . Ni . . .?'

The courier's voice tailed off as she struggled with the unfamiliar Christian name, and, for the hundredth time in her life, Neeve rued the fact that her parents had chosen to call her something so unusual. True, she had alleviated the problems it caused by adopting the phonetic spelling of the name, but on official documents it was still written out in all its tongue-twisting glory: Niamh.

'Neeve,' she said helpfully, turning to the girl, who was frowning at the slip of paper in her hand. 'It's Irish and can be a bit tricky to pronounce if you've not come across it before.'

'Neeve,' the girl repeated carefully. 'You're right, I haven't seen it before, but it's nice.' She smiled, slipping back into her customary guise of brisk efficiency. 'Well, Miss Roberts, I'm sure you'll be pleased to learn that a taxi has arrived for you at last. I'm sorry about the delay, but it appears there has been a mix-up somewhere. We had been told that your booking had been cancelled.'

There was a hint of curiosity in her expression, and Neeve's nicely shaped lips tightened. There had been no mix-up! She knew who had tried to cancel the booking without even having the courtesy to consult with her first. It had been one of the reasons why she had been so determined to make the trip despite all the well-meaning advice from her friends at the library where she worked.

Roger Grantly had already disrupted her well-ordered, carefully laid plans by eloping with a woman old enough to be his mother three weeks before he and Neeve were due to be married, but there was no way he was doing her out of this holiday as well!

There was little she could say, however, without going into all the unsavoury details, so Neeve just smiled non-committally and picked up her case to follow the courier to where the taxi was waiting.

'Right, that seems to be it, then. Have a good holiday, Miss Roberts. I'm sure the weather will pick up for you soon.' With a wave of her hand the girl ran back inside, obviously glad to get Neeve, and all the problems she had apparently caused by turning up, off her hands at last.

Neeve watched her go, a strange little ache starting in the pit of her stomach. So this was it, then, the start of the holiday she'd planned and saved for for the past two years. It was to have been the adventure of a lifetime, the opening chapter of a new life, all neatly mapped out in strict chronological order: a wedding, a honeymoon, a neat little suburban semi and, in time, the regulation two point two children.

So where had it all gone wrong? Why, when she had tried so hard to play it safe, had she ended up on the other side of the world, alone, with all those carefully laid plans in tatters?

If the weather had been a disappointment, then the villa more than made up for it. Dropping her case on the mat by the front door, she walked into the huge airy living-room and looked round with a growing appreciation, loving the contrasting mix of white walls and dark wood, the glowing colours of the rugs strewn across the tiled floor. The travel firm had extolled the Villa Ferma as a place of quiet luxury and, moving from one tastefully decorated room to another, Neeve found herself agreeing with every word.

Delighted, she walked into the small, compact kitchen and ran a glance round the neat expanse of cupboards before opening the fridge door, her eyes widening as she looked inside. The brochure had mentioned something about a starter pack of essential groceries being left in the villa, but she had never expected anything as generous as this vast assortment of cheeses and cooked meats, the array of fruits and vegetables which crammed every shelf. From the look of it she wouldn't need to shop for a week!

Smiling at her sudden upsurge in fortune, she went back to collect her case, then stopped. This was a holiday, after all. The first holiday she'd had in several years, and despite its inauspicious start she had every intention of enjoying it. So, from this minute on she was going to do all the things she *wanted* to do and leave all the dreary jobs, like unpacking, until later. Now number one on her list was a long hot bath!

With a defiant glance at the abandoned case, she turned right round and headed for the bathroom, kicking off her shoes and discarding her jacket as she went. Next came the pretty white silk blouse, closely followed by the wisp of lace satin which masqueraded as a bra. Laughing at such wanton sluttishness, she paused in the bathroom doorway, and slipped off her skirt and dropped it on to the floor then unhooked the fine silk stockings and draped them artistically round the shiny brass doorknob in a cobwebby coil.

She'd spent a fortune on her wedding trousseau, and some little devil nagging inside her head had insisted she should wear the silks and satins which felt so good against her skin. It was doubtful if Roger, with his rather prudish outlook, would have appreciated them anyway!

Turning on the taps, she filled the huge corner bath with steaming water, tossing in a large handful of the pale green bath crystals she found on a shelf in the vanity unit and inhaling their perfume as she stepped into the water. Pulling the pins out of her hair, she let the long, toffee-coloured strands slide round her shoulders and drift on the bubbles. Her eyes closed and she relaxed, letting the heat soak into her body. Bliss!

The shock of hearing the front door being slammed and of footsteps crossing the tiled living-room floor was so great that she sank abruptly and came up spitting mouthfuls of frothy water. Wide-eyed, Neeve stared at the half-open door, her heart pounding wildly when she heard the footsteps slow, then stop, then start again, heading straight for the bathroom.

Panic rose inside her, making her feel dizzy, but determinedly she forced the faintness away. This was no time to faint. She had to do something. She couldn't just sit there naked as the day she was born until heaven knew who came in through the door!

With some vague idea of covering herself with one of the huge bath-towels hanging on the rack, Neeve half rose from the water, then froze when the door was abruptly pushed open. For a stunned moment her eyes met those of the man standing in the doorway, then, with a cry of alarm, she sank back into the water and buried herself in the bubbles right up to the tip of her nose.

'Well, well, and what have we here? I had an idea Greg was up to something, but I never imagined it would be anything like this!'

Eyes huge, Neeve stared at the tall, dark-haired man standing in the doorway, the lacy wisps of her bra and one stocking dangling from the tips of his long fingers. Deep down she knew there must be something she could say, some sort of words, some snappy, witty little phrases just *made* for an occasion like this, but for the dumb life of her she couldn't think what they were!

Perspiration beaded on her brow, trickled down her neck to run between her breasts, but Neeve ignored it. With a final frantic tug she managed to get her skirt up over her damp thighs, then started to fumble with the tiny pearl buttons on the blouse, cursing fluently when she came to the end of the row and found she had one over.

Beyond the closed bathroom door she could hear the man moving about, followed by a sudden silence which was far more unnerving. While he was moving around she had some idea where he was; now she had no idea what he was up to!

Giving the blouse up as a bad job, she took a deep breath. The last thing she wanted to do was go out there and face him again, but she couldn't stay cowering in the bathroom all night. She had to find out what he wanted and then get rid of him . . . fast!

Cautiously she edged the door open and peered out, but there was no sign of him lurking in the shadows, no sign of him anywhere, in fact. With a sinking feeling of fear crawling round her stomach, she crept into the living-room then nearly jumped out of her skin when a deep voice spoke almost directly behind her.

'I think I prefer what you were wearing before. Far more fetching.'

Neeve spun round, her face flushing as she saw the man sprawled in the armchair, his eyes running assessingly up over the slender curves of her body with an expression in their depths which could only be classed as 'knowing'. It was blatantly obvious what he was referring to, and she cursed herself for having had neither the presence of mind nor turn of speed to sink in those bubbles a shade faster!

'So. . . how much was Greg prepared to pay you to come trailing out here? I knew he was planning something when I spoke to him earlier on today, but I must admit I never expected him to go this far.'

Neeve stared blankly at him, her brow furrowing. She seemed to have lost the thread somewhere along the line, and now it was difficult to pick it up again and weave any kind of sense out of his words.

'I'm sorry, but I have no idea what you're talking about.' Her voice sounded hoarse, and she swallowed hard to ease the tension which was knotting her vocal chords into ribbons of steel. 'I don't know anyone called Greg.'

'Oh, come on, lady! Why pretend? I know he's behind this little scheme. Another one of his crazy ideas to, quote, "Get you out of yourself, Nick." Look, I don't mean to be a killjoy, but the last thing I need right now is company, female or any other kind.' He raised the glass he was holding and took a long swallow, his eyes meeting Neeve's with something in their depths which made a shiver dance its way along her spine. 'No disrespect to you, sweetheart. I'm sure you're good at your job, and I really did enjoy that sample of what's on offer, but it was my leg that was injured. The rest of me is working just fine, so I don't need any of your... therapy.'

Therapy? What on earth was he on about? What kind of ther——? Neeve gasped as it suddenly dawned on her exactly what he *had* meant!

'Why, you...you...!' She couldn't seem to get her tongue to work to unravel all the furious retorts twisting inside her head, and before she could sort them all out he held his hand up, putting down the glass while he dug his wallet out of his pocket.

'Listen, I can understand your being annoyed. Nobody likes to make a wasted journey, and I know you have a living to earn the same as the rest of us. So how about another fifty on top of what Greg already paid you? And we won't say anything to him about your going straight back home.'

He held a folded wad of notes out to her. For one long, incredulous minute Neeve stared at it before reaching out to take it from his hand. Slowly, deliberately, she fanned the notes and counted them, ignoring the cynical smile curving his hard mouth as he sat and watched.

'Now that's what I call a sensible girl. Just give me a couple of minutes to finish this drink then I'll see about getting you a taxi back to the airport. You shouldn't have any trouble at this time of the year getting a seat, and I expect Greg will have given you a return tick—— What the hell are you doing?'

Utter astonishment crossed his face as Neeve held the money at arm's length and carefully ripped the notes first into halves then into quarters and then into a dozen tiny pieces. Screwing the pieces into a tight ball, she flung them back at him, her eyes sparkling with fury. Never in the whole twenty-four years of her life had she been so insulted! Hands on hips, she glared down at him, too incensed to notice the way his eyes had darkened with an anger equal to her own.

'For the last time, I have no idea who you are, or who Greg is, or why you should imagine that he

has sent you *me* as a present! All I do know is that
you are not sitting there insulting me any longer. I
am calling the police!'

She swung round to march to the telephone
standing on a small table near the door, then gasped
in alarm as he came to his feet and caught her by
the arm, his long fingers biting into her flesh.

'Don't you threaten me, lady!' he ground out,
his face all hard angles, his dark eyes burning with
a terrifying fire. 'I don't know what your little game
is, but there is no way you are standing there
shooting your mouth off just because I refuse to
succumb to your *charms*!' He sliced a look over
her, a taunting smile twisting his mouth which made
Neeve struggle even harder. 'Is that it? Have I insulted your ego by refusing what was so temptingly
displayed before? Well, I've always been willing to
oblige a lady, and I'd hate for you to leave here
thinking your charms are fading.'

He hauled her to him before she had chance to
realise what he meant, clamping a hand at the back
of her head while he took her mouth, his lips forcing
hers apart with a harsh brutality which terrified her.
Desperately she tried to turn her head and free her
mouth from the rough assault, but with his fingers
twined in her long hair it was impossible to move
an inch. Pushing against his chest with her hands,
she tried to force him away from her, but he was
far too strong and just pulled her even closer,
wrapping his free arm round her like a vice. The
only part of her she could move was her legs, and
Neeve did what any sensible girl would do in the

circumstances—tried to knee him in the groin, but he was so much taller than she was that she only succeeded in catching him a glancing blow against his thigh. However, the effect was staggering.

His whole body stilled, the muscles contracting in a violent spasm so that she was crushed against him, scarcely able to breathe. Then, as though it were happening in slow motion, he started to crumple.

With a startled cry of fear, Neeve wrenched herself free and stepped back, watching with huge, incredulous eyes as he reeled backwards and collapsed on to the chair. His face was ashen, his breathing short and laboured, and for several minutes she just stood and stared at him in utter astonishment. Heaven only knew, she wasn't a big girl—a mere hundred and fourteen pounds of slender female—but if she could have this sort of effect on six feet of solid muscle with only that little tap on the leg then maybe she was missing her vocation by working in the library. With a bit of training, she could conquer the world!

Her euphoria was short-lived, however, when the man started to groan softly under his breath and her eyes darkened with the first stirrings of guilt. Incredible though it seemed, she must really have hurt him. Hesitantly, she stepped forwards, her hand reaching towards him, then leapt back in alarm as his eyes opened and he glared furiously at her.

'Don't you dare touch me!' he ordered grimly, levering himself up on the chair, his face going even paler at the effort it cost him. 'If you know what's good for you, lady, then just get the hell out of here right now before I manage to get back on my feet!'

Neeve turned to go, actually took the first few hurried steps towards the front door, before it suddenly dawned on her what she was doing. She swung round, her eyes raking over him with an answering fury.

'I think you have that all wrong,' she bit back. 'If anyone is leaving here then it is you, not me. You might have overlooked the fact, but I haven't. You're trespassing!'

'Me?' He tried to stand up then fell back, perspiration beading his forehead and upper lip, glistening against the pallor of his skin. He closed his eyes for a moment as though summoning up strength then spoke again a shade more calmly. 'I don't know what sort of game you are playing, but if there is anyone trespassing here then it is you.'

Neeve snorted in disgust and folded her arms across her chest, refusing to give in to the faint but insistent sympathy she felt for the way he was obviously suffering. This was no time to let a sensitive nature get the better of inbred common sense.

'I fail to see how *I* am trespassing. I have rented this villa for the next few weeks and, in case you've forgotten, was quite happily minding my own business getting settled in when you walked in on me!'

His lips twitched, curving ever so slightly into a line of mockery. 'Oh, I've not forgotten. Frankly, I'd say that the sight of you in—or rather, almost

out of—that bath is one that will stay with me for
some time to come.'

'Ooh!' Angered as much by giving him such an
opening as by what he'd said, Neeve swung round
and marched across the room before marching back
and glowering at him.

'That's it! I've had it. I'm tired, I'm hungry and
all I want is for you to tell me what you're doing
here, and leave!'

'I'm sorry to disappoint you but I'm not going
anywhere. I've been staying here for the past couple
of weeks and I have every intention of remaining
here for the next two!'

'What? Oh, but you can't!'

'Oh, but I can.' He sat up, his long fingers
kneading the muscle at the top of his thigh. He grimaced as though it was agony, but some of the
pallor seemed to have left his face. He looked up,
his dark eyes meeting hers. 'Look, lady, I don't
know what the hell is going on, but obviously
there's been some kind of mistake made.'

'Too right there has, but not by me!' Refusing
to give an inch, although her heart was pounding
wildly in nervous apprehension, Neeve met the flat
gaze, wondering how anyone could show as little
expression as he did. His eyes were very dark,
almost black, heavily lashed and with dark circles
underneath them, and looking into them was like
looking into a darkened mirror. She could see
herself reflected in their depths, but nothing else,
no hint of what was going on inside his head, and
it made her quite uneasy.

When he started to rise from the chair she stepped back then instinctively put out her hand to steady him when he staggered.

'I can manage,' he ground out between narrowed lips. He levered himself to his feet and picked up the glass, moving slowly and with obvious difficulty as he carried it across to a trolley laden with bottles. He poured himself a generous measure of whisky and drank it neat before turning to look back at Neeve, who was watching him warily, ready to run at the first sign of trouble.

'All this bickering is getting us nowhere. Let's start from the beginning, shall we? You say that you have never heard of Greg, and that he didn't send you here on one of his wild schemes?'

'No,' she snapped.

'So now that we have established that then let's move on to exactly what you are doing here.'

'I already told you. I've rented the villa for the next two weeks.'

'But are you sure it's this one? There must be hundreds of villas on the island, so are you certain that you've come to the right place?' He spoke slowly and clearly, as though addressing a slightly backward child, and Neeve's mouth tightened into a mean line of irritation.

'Quite sure. I have the booking confirmation *and* the keys in my bag if you want to see them. Villa Ferma for two weeks starting from the fifteenth of October.'

He took another swallow of the drink then set the glass down, running a hand wearily over his hair to push it back from his forehead.

'Then it seems there has been some sort of a mix-up. Still, it's easily remedied, and I'm sure the travel firm will be able to find you alternative accommodation. How about a drink while I get on to the representative and work something out?'

There wasn't a trace of uncertainty in his deep voice, not the smallest indication that he expected her to refuse, but was he in for a surprise! She'd been through too much already just getting here today to meekly turn round and slink off with her tail between her legs. The villa was hers for the next two weeks, and she had the paperwork to prove it. No one, not Roger, not all her well-meaning friends, and definitely not this man, was going to cheat her out of her holiday!

'No!' Her voice rang out loud and clear, and she saw him hesitate in picking up the glass. He glanced back at her, his eyes narrowed.

'You don't drink?'

'No. I mean, yes, I do drink, but no I do not want one while you ring the representative because I have no intention of leaving here!'

He stiffened, turning fully to face her, something about the way he stood menacing, and Neeve felt a quiver run down to her toes. Although he was leanly built, verging on gaunt, really, there was something remarkably intimidating about his height and the set of his powerful shoulders. Dressed

casually in black jeans and black sweater, with his
dark hair falling heavily across his brow and his
black eyes studying her with that flat intensity, he
looked like the devil incarnate, and only sheer frustration at what she'd suffered these past weeks made
Neeve face up to him.

'I don't know who made the mistake and I really
don't care. All I do know is that I have booked this
villa for a holiday, and have every intention of
staying here!'

'Have you? Well, I hate to be the one to disappoint you, lady, but there's the little matter of first
come first served, and as I was here first let me
make it quite plain that I intend to stay.'

'And I booked this holiday over two years ago!
So if it's a case of who has priority on his side then
it's me.'

'Two years? No one books a holiday that far in
advance!' There was open disbelief in his voice, and
Neeve reacted immediately to it.

'They do if it's their honeymoo——' Too late she
realised what she was saying and stopped, one hand
raising to cover her mouth, but the words had
already escaped.

'What did you say?' He came towards her,
pinning her with a hard stare, his face all bones and
angles. 'Did you say honeymoon? My God, is that
what that little paper-chase of undies was for...the
eager bridegroom?' He laughed harshly, sweeping
a glance round the room before turning back to

study the heated curve of her cheeks with mockery. 'So where is he, then?'

Neeve licked her dry lips, wishing the ground would open up and swallow her. 'Who?'

'The blushing bridegroom, of course. Who else?' He smiled coldly. 'Don't tell me he's doing the gentlemanly thing and taking a walk while you get ready for him?'

'No.' Her voice was low, a faint rasp of sound, but he heard her.

'Then what is he doing? That's all we need now to complete this whole fiasco, isn't it—for him to come rushing in here demanding to know what's going on?'

'That's not going to happen.'

'No? Why not? Surely you haven't managed to quarrel already, have you? Though I must admit I can understand how it would be very easy to start a fight with someone of your disposition.'

That stung, and Neeve reacted to it. 'Who are you to make comments about my disposition? You've hardly been Prince Charming! But the answer is no, we haven't quarrelled.'

It was the truth, of course, though not for the reasons he would expect. She and Roger hadn't quarrelled, hadn't exchanged even a cross word. That's what made it all so much worse.

'Then where is he? I shall start fearing the worst soon if you don't tell me—start thinking that you've done something to him.'

'He...he isn't here.' She sort of muttered the words, and he frowned, bending closer to her.

'Pardon?'

'He isn't here.'

'Obviously. But where is he?'

Suddenly it was all too much: Roger's defection, the embarrassment of having to cancel the wedding amid all the gossip and speculation, and now this horrible confrontation. Tears welled into her eyes, but impatiently she brushed them away as she glared back at him.

'Texas!' she spat out as though the word was burning her lips. 'He's in Texas with his new rich ladyfriend. The wedding never took place, but believe me, the honeymoon is going to!'

CHAPTER TWO

DAWN broke slowly, sending the first pale rays of light into the room, but Neeve was already awake.

She rolled over, balling the pillow beneath her cheek as she tried to work out what she should do, how she could face that man again, and groaned. He must think she was crazy, shouting at him and then rushing off into the bedroom like that. It wasn't her usual way of behaving, but, there again, nothing that had happened these past few weeks had been usual.

She closed her eyes as she let the memories come flooding back, feeling again that wave of shame and embarrassment she had felt when she'd received that letter from Roger. Maybe it would have been easier if he'd had the courage to come and tell her to her face that he wouldn't marry her, but he hadn't. The letter, all carefully written in his precise hand, had arrived on the mat with no forewarning. At first Neeve had thought it was some kind of a joke, although she had failed to see the funny side of it. But after she had rung his home and spoken to his mother, she had soon realised that the joke was on her because she had been the only one not to realise what was happening.

For three years she and Roger had gone out together, yet she had never really known him—she couldn't have, not when he could do such a thing without her being the tiniest bit suspicious. To her mind Roger had been everything she'd ever wanted in a man: quiet, dependable, aware of his responsibilities. If he hadn't made her heart beat faster, then so what? It wasn't passion that she was looking for from life, not that wild abandonment one read about in books, but good old-fashioned, solid reliability. But obviously she'd made a huge great error in judgement, because Roger had been looking for something entirely different!

The sound of bedsprings creaking from the adjoining bedroom made her eyes fly open, and she glared at the dividing wall. She had barely slept a wink all night yet every time she'd been on the verge of dropping off that man had awoken her with his tossing and turning. She'd been sorely tempted to hammer on the wall and tell him to keep the noise down, but some inbuilt sense of caution had warned her not to push her luck that far. Now as she listened she could hear the sound of the shower running, and she was suddenly beset by an attack of nerves. A sleepless night was the very least of her problems when she still had the really thorny one of how to get him out of the house to contend with, because, come what may, she was still determined to have the holiday she'd booked and paid for.

She lay in bed listening until eventually silence fell over the house. Tossing back the sheet, she climbed out of bed and pulled on a robe then eased the door open and crept along to the kitchen, taking

rapid stock of the cup and saucer lying on the
counter, the faint aroma of coffee that lingered in
the air. Obviously he had breakfasted, but where
was he now? It seemed too much to hope that he
had left and that she wouldn't have to confront him
again.

As quickly as possible, she checked the rooms,
only breathing a sigh of relief when she found them
empty. She returned to the living-room, and opened
the patio doors wide while she drew in a few deep
breaths of sweet, fresh air, then nearly choked when
she caught sight of him slouched in one of the
padded sun-loungers.

Hearing the sudden explosion of sound, he
turned his head and smiled mockingly at her. 'Surprised to see me?' he asked softly, watching the
colour flow up her cheeks. 'I don't know why.
Surely you didn't think I would leave you here all
alone?'

That was exactly what she had thought, or rather
hoped, but Neeve had no intention of admitting it.
Playing for time, she walked to the edge of the
veranda and stared out at the shelving beach with
its gritty grey sand leading down to the turquoise-
green sea. Yesterday's miserable weather had lifted
but the wind was still fresh, tugging playfully at the
folds of her robe and twisting the long strands of
her hair round her face in silken disarray. Looping
a wayward strand behind her ear, she turned back
to face him, forcing a cool note to her voice.

'I had no idea what your plans were.'

'Of course not, but I'd be failing in my duties as a host if I didn't do everything in my power to see that you get your new accommodation sorted out.'

'My new—now look here, Mr...' She stopped to give him time to supply his name.

'Barclay,' he said slowly. 'Nick Barclay.' And Neeve had the funniest feeling that he was somehow reluctant to part with the information, though for the life of her she couldn't imagine why.

'Well, Mr Barclay, you may have some idea in your head that things have changed since last night, but I'm afraid you're mistaken. This house is mine! I have rented it for the next two weeks and I intend to stay in it!'

'It's you who are mistaken, sweetheart! I might have been willing to make allowances for you last night because you were obviously upset, but believe me, lady, I——'

'Roberts,' she interrupted through gritted teeth. 'The name is Neeve Roberts—not lady, not sweetheart, and not any of the other names you keep on calling me!'

'I don't give a damn what your name is! You're not going to be here long enough for it to matter.' He stood up, and despite herself Neeve stepped back, something about the grimness of his expression making her wary.

'So far I have been very reasonable about your coming in here, invading my privacy. I had intended to help you sort out this mess, but why should I bother wasting my time? You know where the telephone is so I suggest you use it to make a

few calls to arrange alternative accommodation for
yourself. But let's get this straight, once and for all,
Miss Roberts; I am going for a swim now, and when
I get back I don't want to find any sign of you here!
Is that quite clear?'

He strode off without waiting for an answer,
favouring his right leg as he went down the steps
leading to the private beach, leaving Neeve staring
after him in stunned disbelief. Did he really think
he could order her around like that? He must do,
but he was going to find out very quickly that he
was wrong; no chauvinistic male was going to run
her life and tell her what to do after all she'd been
through recently!

Incensed by such cavalier treatment, she stood
and watched as he strode across the sand, only
pausing long enough to shed the cotton trousers
and T-shirt he'd been wearing over dark swimming
trunks before wading into the water and swimming
strongly out to sea. For several minutes, Neeve
stood and glared at the dark head bobbing against
the blue waves, then went and sat down on the
lounger, her lips compressed into a thin line of
anger.

As far as she could see she had two options: she
could either do as he had told her to and leave, or
she could do exactly as she'd been planning on
doing for the past two years and have her holiday.
Frankly, it wasn't difficult to decide which one to
choose! But if she did intend to stay in the villa,
then how was she going to get rid of him?

Smiling nastily, Neeve ran through a list of
possible solutions before sighing sadly as she
realised that she had to be sensible. Tempting
though the idea of lacing his coffee with arsenic
was, the most sensible thing to do was so ridiculously simple that she almost hesitated to choose
it. While he was out there swimming, why didn't
she just pack his bags and leave them outside on
the veranda then lock the door? With that nice crisp
piece of paper in her bag giving her the tenancy of
the villa for the next two weeks, she had the law
well and truly on her side.

Grinning at the thought of Nick Barclay's face
when he got back and found his bags on the step,
she stood up and cast a quick glance out to sea to
check that she had enough time to put her plan into
action. She frowned, moving to the edge of the
veranda as she swept another look over the glittering water, but there was no sign of that dark
head. Suddenly he reappeared, and she half turned
to hurry inside when something about the jerky,
unco-ordinated way he was moving stopped her.
Then, as she watched, he disappeared again beneath the waves, and with a sickening feeling of
fear she realised he was in trouble.

She raced down the steps and on to the beach,
tossing the robe on to the sand as she dived into
the water. There was no time to worry about the
scantiness of the lacy teddie she was wearing, no
time to worry about anything except getting to the
man who was struggling wildly as he surfaced again.
The swell was heavier than it had looked from the

shore, but she battled on, keeping her head low as she cut through the water and finally reached him.

Grasping him by the shoulder, she attempted to turn him on to his back to tow him back to shore, but he was still struggling wildly, his arms threshing the water. The back of his hand caught her a stinging blow across the cheek, and she sank, coughing and spitting water as she surfaced again.

'Stop it, Nick!' she shouted, catching hold of his arm and hanging on like a limpet. 'You'll drown us both.'

His head came round, the black eyes barely focused, his mouth twisted in pain. 'Cramp,' he managed to grit out. 'My leg . . . cramp.'

A wave caught him full in the face, and he started to go under again, but Neeve held him up, treading water as she supported them both against the force of the swell.

'Just do as I tell you. Don't struggle.'

She must have got through to him because he stopped fighting, letting her turn him so that she could clamp an arm beneath his chin before starting to swim back to the shore. He tried to help her, using his hands as paddles and kicking his good leg, but she was completely exhausted by the time her heels scraped the bottom. On hands and knees she hauled him as far out of the water as she could, then collapsed beside him, her chest heaving with exertion, dots of light dancing behind her closed lids. She could hear the rasping whine of his laboured breathing keeping time with hers, but it was too much of an effort to turn and look at him.

'Thank you.'

His hand brushed her bare thigh, and she
managed to lift her head from the sand, tossing
back the matted length of hair from her face. Their
eyes were on a level, and she felt a heated jolt run
through her at the first sign of warmth she'd ever
seen in their dark depths.

'Thank you . . . Neeve,' he repeated, his voice
hoarse and raspy. His eyelids flickered shut, and
Neeve turned away, letting her head fall back
against the warm grittiness of the sand, feeling her
heart pounding in a new rhythm she didn't understand, and didn't want to. Nick Barclay had insulted her, ridiculed her and kissed her until she
was breathless, but nothing he had done so far
frightened her as much as her own reaction to that
unexpected hint of warmth in his eyes!

Shaken by the discovery, she lay on the beach
letting the heat of the sun dry her skin until she
heard him starting to move. She rolled over, eyeing
him warily as she wondered what was going to
happen next, but he merely held his hand out to
her, a faint smile curving his lips.

'Come on, time to get you inside before you
finish up with sunstroke. That would be a fine
reward for risking your life out there rescuing me.'

There was a teasing note in his deep voice which
was irresistible for being so totally unexpected, and
Neeve couldn't help smiling back at him. She sat
up to offer him her hand, her eyes running automatically up the length of his body, and couldn't

hide the gasp which sprang to her lips when she caught sight of the livid scar on his right leg.

Stunned by the sight, her eyes traced over the cruel disfigurement which ran in a horseshoe shape from his inner thigh to skim the top of his knee before curving back to disappear into the leg of his swimming-trunks below his right hip.

'Not a pretty sight, is it? I apologise that you should be subjected to it!'

His voice was stiff with a mixture of pride and anger, and Neeve realised that her unwitting re-action had offended him deeply.

'I'm sorry. I didn't mean to——'

'We'd better get inside.' He cut her off, taking her hand to haul her abruptly to her feet, his face closed and shuttered, his eyes once more devoid of expression. Without waiting for her, he strode on ahead, his back ramrod straight despite the ob-vious pain he was suffering from his leg.

Neeve blinked, pushing back her hair, won-dering why she felt the most ridiculous urge to cry. She followed him up the path and into the house, going straight to the bathroom to strip off the teddie, which felt sticky from its immersion in sea water, before stepping under the shower. The warm water flowed over her skin, easing the ache from her muscles, but nothing could ease the ache from her heart for causing Nick such pain. It had just been the shock, that was all—the shock of seeing the scar, and her reaction had been instinctive, not prompted by revulsion as he obviously thought. Against the tanned skin of his muscular thigh the

scar had been vividly noticeable, the freshly healed
flesh both raw and angry-looking. No wonder she
had felled him last night with that blow; it must
have been agony for him, and she only wished she
could apologise, but she had the feeling that he
wouldn't want to hear any apologies she might
make when he was obviously so bitterly aware of
how it looked.

Back in her room, she found clean underclothes
and a pair of cool cotton Bermuda shorts and
matching top, and slipped them on then brushed
her hair back into a pony-tail. There was a knock
at the door, and she hurried to answer it, feeling
her heart thumping when she found Nick standing
outside the door.

'There's coffee made if you want some.' He
turned to go without another word, and instinctively Neeve caught his arm to stop him. He might
not want to hear any apologies she had to make,
but she was going to try!

'Nick, about what happened before on the
beach...'

'Forget it,' he said shortly, his black eyes slicing
a look over her troubled face before dropping
meaningfully to where her hand was resting on his
arm. Neeve let her hand drop, but stood her ground,
refusing to let him freeze her out so easily.

'I can't forget it. I offended you and I apologise.'

'It isn't the first time that a woman has found
the sight of it more than she could stomach, and I
doubt it will be the last, so, as I said, forget it. I'm
sure I'll learn to live with other people's reactions.

Now if you'll excuse me the coffee will be getting cold.'

It was obvious that he had no intention of listening, so Neeve let him go, watching the proud lift of his head as he limped back to the kitchen. He hadn't been limping like that earlier on, so obviously the morning's mishaps had taken their toll on more than just his pride. Why had he taken such a risk and gone swimming out so far when his leg was barely healed?

However, curious as she was to know why Nick Barclay had acted so foolishly, she knew that she had a far more pressing matter to attend to. Somehow she had to make him see sense and accept the fact that the villa was hers now, but how she was going to do that was beyond her. Mulling over the problem, she made her way to the kitchen and stopped in the doorway, unsure of where to begin. Nick glanced up, raising the mug of coffee to his lips to take a long swallow as he watched her over the rim. Colour flared into her cheeks as she felt the assessing gaze run up the length of her bare legs, and she walked hurriedly over to the coffee-pot and busied herself pouring a cup of the fragrant brew to hide her sudden confusion.

'Have you managed to find alternative accommodation yet?'

Neeve jumped when he spoke, splashing hot coffee on to the back of her hand. The hot droplets stung, and she put down the jug, sucking the angry little spots while she flashed him a look of open irritation.

'No, of course I haven't. I haven't had time. I was too busy rescuing you from drowning, if you remember?' There was more than a trace of sarcasm in her reply, and his eyes narrowed but he spoke quite calmly.

'Then I suggest that you make a start when you have finished that coffee.'

Well, what had she expected? That he would be so grateful to her that he would offer to do the gentlemanly thing and leave? No, she had never expected that for a moment, but she had never expected such brusqueness either! Anger whipped a froth of colour into her cheeks, and she swung round, leaving the untouched mug of coffee standing on the counter.

'And what if I refuse? What will you do then? Throw me out bodily?' She laughed scornfully, letting her eyes drop quite deliberately to his leg. 'I doubt if you're up to that, do you?'

His face went rigid, every hard bone starkly outlined under the lean, tanned flesh of his cheeks, the hand holding the mug clenching. 'Don't push your luck, lady,' he said tautly, his black eyes boring holes into her. 'You could find yourself regretting it.'

'Could I indeed? Well, I suppose I'll have to take your word for it, Mr Barclay, although I fail to be convinced.' She turned round, quite deliberately setting her back towards him, feeling the back of her neck prickling from the heat of his furious glare. Deep down she knew she was being foolish to push him like this, but for once in her life she didn't care. All her adult life she had been sensible, and look where it had got her! Now all the anger and resentment she'd held in check since Roger's defection reared up and, whether it was fair or not, Nick Barclay was going to bear the brunt of it!

The sound of a chair scraping against the tiles brought her spinning round, but he made no move to approach her and take her up on the taunting challenge to eject her bodily. He stared coldly at her, his face set into a mask of contempt. 'I can see why that boyfriend of yours ran out on a shrew like you. He had a lucky escape, but if you think you can practise sharpening your tongue on me then think again! I want you out of here now, and I don't give a damn where you go or what happens to you!'

He swung round to walk stiffly to the door, but she wasn't about to let him walk out after saying that! Without stopping to consider the wisdom of her actions, Neeve snatched up the mug of coffee and hurled it after him. It bounced off his shoulder and crashed against the wall, spraying coffee everywhere as it shattered. For a moment there was absolute silence, then Nick turned round, and she caught her breath at the naked fury on his face.

'You little bitch. It's about time that someone taught you a lesson!'

'And who might that someone be? You? Huh!' She hadn't wanted to say that, hadn't *consciously* thought out the most explosive answer she could have found. The words had just leapt out of their own volition, and now she went cold as she saw the gleam in his black eyes when he moved back into the room with an intent and purpose which were unmistakable.

With a cry of alarm, Neeve leapt back, setting the barrier of the table between them, but it seemed very little protection when he looked angry enough to commit murder! She scuttled round the table, dodging back to elude his hand, then made a dash for the door, reaching it just a split second before he did. On winged feet she raced through the house and fumbled with the catches on the front door. She could hear him coming after her, cursing under his breath as he was forced to move more slowly than he would have liked because of his leg. The door refused to give, the brass bolt at the top so stiff that she couldn't manage to draw it back with her fumbling fingers, and she whimpered in fear. Suddenly the telephone rang and she snatched it up, praying that the caller would understand her plea for help.

'Hel——!'

'Hello?' The voice was male, holding a definite note of surprise as though he hadn't expected a woman to answer.

'Give me that!' Nick came up beside her and tried to take the receiver from her hand, but Neeve held on to it as if it were a lifeline.

'Hello,' she said urgently, swinging away to cradle it against her ear as he made another lunge to snatch it from her. 'Can you hear me? I need hel——'

'Yes, sorry. I was just surprised when you answered. Nick is a dark horse. I only wish that he'd told me about you before I——' He broke off, then continued swiftly, 'Still, not to worry. I'm just pleased to find out that he isn't on his own after all, although he has kept you so secret that I've no idea of your name!'

'Roberts . . . Neeve Roberts,' she responded automatically, glancing sideways at Nick, who was leaning against the wall now with his eyes closed, although she had the nasty feeling that he was merely conserving his energy rather than giving up! The thought brought her up short, and she spoke again, a shade more determinedly. 'Look, I've no idea who you are, but——'

'Greg Barclay, Nick's cousin. He must have mentioned me, surely?'

'Indeed he has, Mr. Barclay!' There was an edge to her voice as she remembered the circumstances, but Greg seemed quite oblivious to it as he continued in the same friendly tone.

'I thought he would have done. Well, Neeve, it's been great talking to you. I had been toying with the idea of flying out there just to keep Nick company and stop him brooding but, now I know you're there with him, I won't need to bother. I don't want to intrude! Tell Nick I rang, will you? And have a great time both of you. Believe me, this is just what he needs to buck him up!'

'Oh, but——' The line went dead, and slowly Neeve replaced the receiver, jumping slightly when Nick spoke abruptly.

'So what did Greg have to say?'

Neeve took a deep breath, mentally preparing herself for whatever might follow, but, surprisingly, apart from a slight grimness to his expression, Nick appeared quite calm.

'Just that he had been thinking about coming out here to join you but that he won't bother now he knows I'm here.'

'Thank heavens!'

He pushed away from the wall and walked back into the living-room, sitting down heavily in one of the chairs. Neeve followed him slowly, keeping a wary distance between them. He seemed calm enough now, granted, but there was no reason to take any unnecessary chances. However, he did nothing to alarm her as he settled back in the chair, an expression of resignation on his face as he looked up at her.

'So, that's it, then—looks as if your wish is about to be granted after all.'

'Pardon?' She frowned, wondering what he meant by the enigmatic statement.

'To stay here at the villa.'

'Stay here? Are you offering to leave?'

He shook his head, his mouth twisting sardonically at her startled expression. 'No, I am not.'

'Then I don't understand.'

'It's quite simple. I don't want Greg or anyone else coming here to, quote, "keep me company". I've had it up to here with all the well-meaning advice, the desire to bring me out of myself. The main reason I came here was to get away from all that and be by myself. I've had three months of people fussing over me, and all I want now is to be on my own! If Greg knows that you are here, then he will scrap any ideas of coming over. So in the circumstances the most sensible thing to do is to make you an offer to share the villa for the next couple of weeks.'

'Share? You . . . and me?'

'Yes.' He swept a hand round the room. 'Face it, the place is plenty big enough for both of us to be here without invading the other's privacy. We can go our separate ways and barely be aware of each other's presence.' He looked up at her, his face suddenly grim. 'And you need have no worries that I will try to take advantage of the situation. The last thing I need right now is that kind of involvement!'

'I . . . I don't know.'

Neeve turned away and walked over to the window, staring out at the glittering view of the bay. For two years now she'd dreamed of being here and enjoying this view, but it should have been in such vastly different circumstances. Now Roger was no longer a part of the picture she'd formed in her mind, and she had accepted the fact even though it still rankled and made up her mind to enjoy the holiday. But was it really wise to accept such a proposal when she knew so little about Nick Barclay, apart from the fact that he had a bad leg and an even worse temper?

'Come on. What have you got to lose? Live dangerously for once in your life, woman!'

There was a taunting note of challenge in his voice, and Neeve's mouth tightened. Live dangerously, indeed! Well, if that injury of his was any example of living dangerously, then she would have to turn the offer down flat!

She swung round to refuse, then stopped abruptly when she caught sight of the expression on his face. Pain, weariness and a strange loneliness were all mirrored fleetingly on his gaunt features, and something strangely warm and unexpected flooded her heart.

'All right,' she said quietly. 'I'll accept your offer and stay.'

'You won't regret it.'

He stood up rather awkwardly and held his hand out to her and, after a brief hesitation, Neeve took it, feeling a tingle of awareness shoot up her arm at the feel of his cool flesh on hers. Abruptly she pulled her hand away and walked out on to the veranda, feeling the coolness of the wind against her heated skin.

All her adult life she had made sensible, rational decisions, so what had prompted her to act so foolishly out of character? The expression on the face of a man she barely knew? She must be mad! All she could hope was that she wouldn't come to regret such folly.

CHAPTER THREE

NEEVE had never suffered from loneliness before. Her parents had always lived their life surrounded by a host of friends and admirers so that she had learned at an early age to treasure those rare moments on her own. Loneliness was the one thing that had never bothered her about coming on this holiday by herself, yet it was bothering her now, and it was all Nick Barclay's fault!

With a sigh she sat up and slid the sunglasses down on to her nose as she stared blankly across the bay. Nick had stated that he would keep out of her way when he had offered to share the house, but she had never imagined that he would be so... *punctilious* about it. It was obvious that he was avoiding her and, although she knew that she should be glad that he was sticking to his word, somehow it irked her that he could so easily dismiss her from his mind when he seemed to occupy such a large part of hers! If she'd been completely on her own then the lack of company wouldn't have bothered her a jot, but the fact that Nick was here, yet so tantalisingly distant, seemed to arouse all these uncharacteristic feelings of loneliness.

Determined to put the wretched man out of her mind once and for all, she shot a glance round the beach then unhooked the top of her bikini and

tossed it on to the sand. It was the first time she
had ever gone topless, and she felt incredibly daring
as she settled down to her sunbathing and felt the
warmth of the sun on her exposed skin. She closed
her eyes and yawned, wriggling down into the soft
cushions.

Nick might be an elusive house-mate, spending
every day well away from the villa, but he had a
nasty habit of making his presence felt when she
least appreciated it. He was a restless sleeper, tossing
and turning, even calling out on occasion, so that
most nights she'd been woken by the sounds coming
from his room. Now the mounting tiredness caught
up with her, and she fell fast asleep.

'My God, woman, are you mad?'

The angry voice cut through the pleasant little
dream she was enjoying, and Neeve murmured in
annoyance, snuggling her head into the cushion to
blot out the irritating sound.

'Wake up! Come on . . . wake up!'

A hand caught her by the shoulder and shook
her roughly, the harsh grip incredibly painful on
her skin. Neeve opened her eyes and blinked
sleepily, then stared at the tall figure looming over
her in confusion.

'Don't you have any sense at all? How long have
you been out here? Just look at yourself!'

Still awash with sleep, Neeve followed the sweep
of his hand, then gasped with horror as she suddenly realised she was lying there half naked. She
sat up abruptly, her hands moving to shield her

breasts from Nick's eyes, then groaned when the top of her head seemed to lift off. Nausea welled in her throat, and she swallowed hard, terrified that she was going to suffer the indignity of throwing up along with everything else.

'Take a deep breath. Slowly now. And another. Come on . . . nice and steady.' Nick crouched down beside her, supporting her throbbing head with a gentle hand while she followed his instructions, and gradually the spasm passed.

'Can you stand up? Here, give me your hand and I'll help you.'

He stood up and held out his hand to her, but there was no way that she was going to relinquish the rather tentative hold she had on modesty by giving him one of her hands! As awkward as a lame duck, she swung her legs over the side of the sunbed, and attempted to stand while still keeping her hands firmly covering her breasts.

'Oh, for heaven's sake!' With a quick jerk, Nick hauled her to her feet, holding her steady as her legs started to buckle as fresh pain sliced through her head.

'Don't do that,' she muttered, forcing the words out through lips which didn't seem to belong to her. 'It makes my head hurt!'

'You deserve to have it hurt! Of all the stupid, idiotic things to do!'

'Do you have to shout? Can't you see I'm ill?'

'Oh, I can see that all right. I couldn't miss it. Frankly, I've never seen that fetching shade of red

on the skin of anything other than a boiled lobster
before!'

Neeve glanced down, squinting as she tried to
focus her eyes to see if the cruel description fitted,
but her head was throbbing so hard that it seemed
impossible to accomplish even that small task.
Wearily she let her head drop forwards, murmuring in relief when it came to rest against something warm and hard and comfortingly solid.

'Do you think you can walk?'

His voice seemed very close, rumbling deeply in
her ear, and she opened one eye a crack, then
blinked when she discovered that she was resting
against his chest. Embarrassment ran through her,
and hurriedly she attempted to straighten up, then
gave it up as a bad job when the whole world started
to tilt.

For a few wobbly seconds she let herself rest
against him, savouring the feel of his firm body,
which felt so marvellously steady when everything
around her seemed to be spinning like a whirligig,
then gasped in alarm when she felt herself being
lifted off the ground.

'Put me down,' she ordered weakly. 'Please,
Nick, put me down before you hurt yourself.'

'I won't hurt myself if you'll keep still and put
your arm round my neck. For heaven's sake,
woman, I'm not going to be driven mad with lust
if I catch a glimpse of your naked body!'

There was such annoyance in his voice that Neeve
did as he'd ordered, sliding her arms around his
neck to brace herself before closing her eyes so that

she wouldn't have to see her own nakedness. Slowly
and with some difficulty, he carried her back to the
house, laying her down on the bed with a heartfelt
sigh of relief.

'Either you weigh a whole lot more than you look
as if you do, or I'm not as fit as I imagined, but,
whichever, I'm glad that bit's over! Now lie there
while I find something to put on that sunburn and
ease your headache. Oh, and try not to get into any
more trouble for a couple of minutes, will you?'

Neeve ignored him, turning her face away as he
shot her a hard look before walking out of the
room. He was a fine one to talk about getting into
trouble when she'd had to rescue *him* from
drowning! However, now was not the time to be
totting up scores; now she had to find something
to put on before he came back!

She sat up and swung her legs over the side of
the bed, taking a deep breath as the nausea rose in
her throat again. Slowly, she stood up, holding on
to the furniture as she made her way towards the
wardrobe, but she'd barely made it halfway before
Nick reappeared, a glass of some cloudy liquid in
one hand and a basin of water in the other.

He set them down on the bedside table, his face
dark with anger as he came back and swept her off
her feet to carry her back to the bed. 'Can't you
ever do what you're told? Now drink this up.' He
propped her up, one arm supporting her shoulders
while he fed her sips of the soluble aspirin, ignoring her half-hearted protests until it had all gone.
'Right, at least you've managed to do that! It will

take a while before it has any effect, but it should ease the worst of your headache. Now let's do something about that sunburn.'

Setting the glass down, he dipped a cloth into the water in the basin then started to sponge her skin, his movements deft and gentle as he ran the cloth over her hot cheeks and down her neck.

Neeve murmured in relief as she felt the cool touch of the cloth, then gasped when he swept it down lower over her breasts. Her hand flew up, her fingers clamping tightly around his wrist to stop him, but he just unfurled her fingers one by one and pushed her hand away.

'This is not the time for any silly ideas about modesty. You have one bad dose of sunburn there, and if you don't want to spend the rest of this holiday in a hospital bed then I suggest you forget all your prudish little scruples and let me get on with the job of cooling you down. Frankly, lady, you've got nothing there that I haven't seen a dozen times before, and in a whole lot better condition!'

He turned away, dipping the cloth into the water again, leaving Neeve gasping in open-mouthed anger. What did he mean 'better condition'? Fair enough, so she wasn't the best endowed of women, but there was nothing *wrong* with her bosom as far as she could see!

Anger raced through her, chasing away the embarrassment, so that she was scarcely aware of Nick running the cloth over the skin on her stomach and legs. When he had finished he picked up the cotton robe lying over the back of a chair and draped it across her.

'Now I suggest that you lie there and try to get some rest. It will help ease that headache, although I doubt it will do much for the sunburn. You are in for an uncomfortable night from the look of it, and you only have yourself to blame. No one but an idiot lies out in the midday sun even at this time of the year, and especially not if they have your fair skin!' He shot her a hard look, his expression altering slightly when he saw the mutinous curve of her mouth. 'Now, now, don't start sulking,' he said silkily, his voice holding a note which made her shoot him a wary glance.

'I am not sulking!' she snapped. 'Why should I be?'

'No reason I can think of...unless I hurt your feelings by what I said before.' He tossed the cloth into the bowl, smiling mockingly as he bent and turned her face up so that she was forced to meet his eyes. 'I was referring to the sunburn before, Neeve. From where I'm standing everything looks to be in first-rate condition apart from that!'

Neeve gasped, pulling her head away, hearing the soft sound of his laughter as he walked out of the room and closed the door. He was the most arrogant, conceited man she'd ever come across if he thought for one second that she cared twopence for his opinion!

She rolled over, burrowing her hot face into the blessed coolness of the pillow, wishing Nick Barclay a million miles away. Yet, strangely, when she did

finally fall asleep, it wasn't how much he annoyed
her that she dreamt about, but how deliciously
soothing his hands had felt on her skin.

It was dark when she woke up. For a few minutes
she lay still, letting her mind drift back to con-
sciousness, then sat up, gasping, when red-hot
needles of pain prickled her skin.

Carefully, she climbed out of the bed and crossed
to the dressing-table, wincing when she switched
on the small lamp and saw the fiery colour staining
her skin. If this was the effect topless sunbathing
could have, then that had been her first and last
shot at it, but, horrible though it looked, she knew
she'd got off pretty lightly, thanks to Nick Barclay's
unexpected arrival and prompt treatment.

The thought of just how he had treated the
sunburn made her feel suddenly even hotter, and
she quickly slipped on a robe before walking to the
door and easing it open just a crack, but the whole
house was silent. With a wry little smile, she made
her way to the kitchen and poured herself a glass
of fruit juice and sipped it thirstily.

The fact that Nick had spared time from his busy
schedule to minister to her didn't mean that she
should expect such attention again. Now that he
had done what he'd obviously felt beholden to do
in the circumstances, he had left to resume his ac-
tivities without a second thought for her. She would
never have expected anything else so it was strange
to realise just how much it hurt.

She rinsed the glass and put it away then walked
through the living-room and on to the veranda. A

light breeze was blowing in from the sea, carrying with it the scent of salt, the coolness of spray. Neeve lifted her hair back from her face, enjoying the feel of it against her heated skin.

'How do you feel now?'

The low-voiced question startled her so much that she spun round, her hand going to her throat to stem the sudden wild pounding of her heart. Now that her eyes had adjusted to the night, she could see Nick sitting in one of the chairs, his long legs crossed at the ankle, his feet propped on the wooden rail. With his black hair and the dark clothing he seemed to favour, he had merged into the shadows so that she'd had no warning that he was there. Now she felt her pulse leap as she saw the gleam in his eyes as he subjected her to an assessing scrutiny which made her suddenly ridiculously conscious of the thinness of the robe.

Hurriedly she turned away, keeping her face averted from that intent gaze which seemed to strip her bare. It was silly to feel this self-conscious after everything that had happened, but she couldn't seem to stop the strange little shivers of awareness which kept dancing down her spine.

'Not too bad. The headache has almost gone, but I still feel very hot and rather sore.' Her voice was just slightly husky, betraying her unease, and she hurried on, 'It was a good job you came back when you did or I think I might have fried!'

He made no attempt to share the small joke, his face very hard as he glared back at her. 'It definitely was! Sunburn isn't a joking matter. Another half-hour and you would have needed hospital treatment!'

'I know. It was a stupid thing to do, and I've learned my lesson. But thank you anyway for...well, for taking care of me. It would probably be far worse now if you hadn't acted so promptly.'

His expression altered subtly, his eyes gleaming in a way that made the hot blood rush to her head in a most disturbing way.

'That was my pleasure, believe me. A real pleasure!' He laughed softly, his mouth curving into a wicked smile which added a roguish charm to his lean face. 'Funny, but I'd swear you were blushing under all that sunburn! Surely my "prompt actions" weren't such a shock to you? After all, it can't have been the first time that a man has seen you naked.'

Neeve gasped, feeling the heat pounding under her already hot skin. 'That is none of your business! If I had paraded naked in front of a whole regiment, then it wouldn't be any of your concern, Nick Barclay!'

He laughed again, making no attempt to hide his amusement this time, a deep flow of sound which carried on the breeze and seemed to envelop her in the sensation of being stroked by a velvet-gloved hand. 'A whole regiment, eh? Now that *would* surprise me! From the opinion I'd formed, I imagined that it had been the first time that any man had laid eyes on you, let alone touched you, but of course I must have been wrong. You were engaged to be married so, although you might act with a virginal modesty, I doubt you can be that!'

How dared he? How dared he…speculate about her virginity, or lack of it! Neeve rounded on him, her hazel eyes spitting furious sparks. 'I'll thank you to keep your opinions to yourself. Just because you helped me this afternoon doesn't mean that you now have the right to start making assumptions about how I conduct my life! What Roger and I did, or didn't do, is none of your business!'

She swung away, not quite sure why she felt so angry about his mocking words. She and Roger hadn't slept together. Not that it had been any conscious decision, more a case of neither of them having felt that it was, well…necessary. Now she refused to stand there and let a stranger speculate on her love-life that way.

She marched across the veranda then stopped dead when Nick rose to his feet and barred her way. She tried to side-step him, but he moved just a split second before she did so that once more she found him in her path.

'Do you mind? I want to go inside!'

'I do mind, as a matter of fact.' He reached out and caught her by the shoulders, his fingers gentle against her sunburnt skin as he held her at arm's length, and for some strange reason Neeve couldn't bring herself to break away from the gentle hold.

'If I have offended you, then I apologise.'

'You do?' Neeve shot him a wary glance, searching for any hint of that mockery again, but he met her eyes with a level look.

'I do. Look, I have a bottle of wine chilling in the fridge, so how about having a glass with me to show there are no hard feelings?'

'Well...' She hesitated, torn between a desire to go storming off just to show him how angry she still was and by the even stronger and totally inexplicable one to stay.

'Come on. Where's the harm in it? Just have a little, since you're still a bit queasy. We're already sharing the villa, so sharing a bottle of wine is no big deal.'

Put like that it seemed ridiculous to refuse, but she still tagged on a proviso, not wanting him to think he could have everything his own way. There was something about Nick Barclay that warned her getting his own way was second nature to him.

'All right, but just the one. I don't have much of a head for drink.'

'Fine.' He rubbed his fingertips lightly down her arms before he let her go in a gesture which should have been nothing more than one of friendship, yet she was aware of the scorching heat from his touch burning hotter than the sunburn.

'You go and sit down, and I'll fetch the bottle.' He turned to walk inside, then paused, his eyes filled with laughter as he shot a glance back over his shoulder. 'Oh, and Neeve, you have my word that I won't make any more personal remarks about your lifestyle even if I find out that a whole army has feasted its eyes on your charms!'

He disappeared inside, leaving her staring after him, not knowing whether to scream with fury or with laughter. From the outset, Nick Barclay had been an unknown quantity, like an iceberg, with nine-tenths of him hidden under the surface. But if the ice was suddenly to melt would she be able to cope with the resulting flood of emotions which threatened to swamp her mind?

Based on the disastrous way her relationship with Roger had ended, she was obviously no authority on men, and Roger had been boringly predictable compared to this man. If she really was the sane and rational woman she had always prided herself on being, then she should go straight back to her room and forget any ideas about sharing this wine!

So how was it, then, that she found herself sitting down in the chair, smoothing her skirts and folding her hands in her lap as she waited for him to come back? Surely this was a fine time to start breaking her own rules about playing it safe... and to start living dangerously!

CHAPTER FOUR

THE wine was deliciously cool. Neeve took another sip from her glass, then pressed it against her cheek, savouring the momentary relief it gave her from the heat of the sunburn. She stared out to sea, forcing herself to concentrate on the lights of a boat which was making its way across the bay, all too aware of the man sitting next to her. He moved suddenly, and she started nervously, but all he did was pick up the bottle of wine from where it was standing in the space between their chairs and refill his glass before offering it to her.

'Another?'

She shook her head, feeling her heart thumping wildly. What had happened now to all those fine ideas about living dangerously? They seemed to have melted away faster than the frost on the wine bottle, leaving her a jittery mass of nerves. She was being ridiculous, acting like this. Nick Barclay had offered her a glass of wine, nothing more, and definitely nothing to make her start jumping every time he moved a muscle!

She drew in a nice long steadying breath, forcing a cool note to her voice. 'One's enough for me, thanks. After all, I'm still recovering, remember. I don't want to end up tipsy. That really would round off a memorable day!'

He set the bottle back down on the floor again before swinging his feet comfortably up on to the rail. 'I don't think there's much danger of that. Two glasses of wine aren't going to get you rip-roaring drunk.'

'Mm, maybe not, but I shall err on the side of caution anyway. Roger always says that...' She stopped dead, burying her face in the glass as she took a gulp of wine, cursing herself for mentioning Roger's name.

'Roger was your fiancé, I take it?'

She nodded, staring blankly out to sea while she waited for the familiar ache to start nagging inside but, surprisingly, she felt nothing.

'What happened between you? You mentioned another woman. Did he dump you for her?'

What had she expected—tact, sympathy, even a touch of delicate diplomacy in asking the question so many others had skirted around? She had no idea, but wasn't it just typical that he should come out with it so baldly! From what she'd discovered about Nick Barclay, tact and diplomacy were two graces he had no use for!

She shot him a hostile stare. 'I don't wish to talk about it.'

He shrugged, lifting his glass to take a long, appreciative swallow of the wine before answering. 'Please yourself, but it seems to me that you could do with letting go rather than bottling it all up inside you.'

'I am not bottling anything up! Just because I don't choose to discuss my private life with ... with a stranger does *not* mean that I'm bottling things up!'

'Oh, we're hardly strangers, surely? Not after to-day's little episode. I can honestly claim to know you far more intimately than a stranger would!'

He was taunting her quite deliberately and, although Neeve knew it, she couldn't help the sudden *frisson* which ran along her spine as she saw the way his eyes ran over her body. Draining the last of the wine from her glass, she reached for the bottle to refill it, too disturbed to remember her previous need for caution.

'Well?' he prompted, and she knew that he would never let the matter drop now unless she gave him some sort of an explanation. Suddenly it seemed easier to comply rather than make an issue out of it and suffer any more of his taunting little comments, which made her feel so strangely vulnerable.

'There's not much to tell. Roger wrote me a letter three weeks before the wedding, telling me that he thought we would be making a huge mistake by going through with it.'

'And you had no inkling that it was going to happen?'

She shook her head, her face clouding as she remembered her confusion, her total inability to make sense of the precise little sentences Roger had written. 'None at all. He'd seemed much the same as always—a bit abstracted, but I put that down to all the overtime he'd been working.' She laughed a trifle bitterly. 'Overtime indeed! Turns out he'd been meeting his "friend" on those nights, and I, like a fool, believed him.'

'You had no reason to believe otherwise, I expect.'

She took a sip of the wine, letting it lie coldly on her tongue before swallowing it down. 'I suppose not, but it didn't stop me feeling a fool once I found out. It seems that everyone apart from me knew what was going on!'

'That's often the case.' There was a hollow ring to his voice, and Neeve shot him a quick look from under her lashes, curious to know what had caused it, but his face was totally impassive. If she wanted to know, then she would have to ask him, but she shied away from doing that. There was something remote about Nick Barclay which precluded any attempts to ask him personal questions.

He seemed to drag himself back to the present, turning his head slightly to level a searching look at her. 'So what happens after this holiday?'

Neeve shrugged, looking down at the glass as she tipped the pale gold wine from side to side. 'Nothing much out of the ordinary. I'll go back to work and just carry on as normal, I expect.'

'You're not going to seek a reconciliation with your fiancé, then?'

'Definitely not! He's made his decision, and that's that as far as I'm concerned!'

'Doesn't sound to me as though you're suffering from a broken heart as much as injured pride, otherwise you'd be eager to try to get him back.'

'How? Even if I wanted to, just tell me how I'd go about doing that? I already told you that he's flown over to America.'

'That's not the other side of the moon! You could always go over there and see if you could work things out between you.'

'No thanks! He had his chance and, as far as I'm concerned, that's it. Roger Grantly is now past history.' She sat up straighter, her face stiff with pride, her eyes sparkling with temper. 'There is no way I'm going running after him. That would only give people even more to talk about, and frankly I've had my fill of being the butt of all the gossip, not to mention the embarrassment, of having to cancel all the arrangements!'

'What upset you most, Neeve, Roger leaving you, or the fact that all your carefully laid plans were ruined?'

'I don't know what you mean,' she snapped, glaring at him.

'Don't you? I think you do. I think if you're really honest with yourself you'll face up to the fact that you aren't as upset about losing Roger as you are about having to start mapping out a new future for yourself.'

'You know nothing at all about me, Nick Barclay, so I hardly think you're qualified to make judgements like that!' She set the glass down with a sharp little clatter, afraid that she would be sorely tempted to throw it at him if he continued in this vein.

He tossed back the rest of his wine, then refilled his glass, looking at her over the rim, and Neeve was hard pushed not to squirm under the force of the steady scrutiny. 'If you mean that I don't have a nice neat biography of you, then fair enough, but I know your type, so I think I can guess fairly accurately how you are feeling right now.'

'My type?' Anger rolled inside her and she sucked in a huge great breath to hold it down. 'And what type is that exactly?'

Her tone was sharply acidic, and she saw him smile as he leaned back in his seat, the light spilling from the open patio doors lending a burnished sheen to his dark hair yet leaving his face deeply shadowed. Only his voice seemed clear, deep and vibrant with barely suppressed amusement as it carried on the still night air.

'Sure you really want to know?'

'Oh, yes! I can hardly wait, believe me. So come along, Mr Know-it-All Barclay; tell me what *type* I am!'

'At a rough guess I'd put you down as being someone extremely cautious by nature. A person who likes to map out her life to the nth degree, and know exactly where she is going so that there are no surprises.'

His perception annoyed Neeve intensely, as did the less than flattering assessment of her character, which made her sound dull as ditch-water. She had always viewed her way of planning life step by careful step as common sense, an understandable reaction against the crazily unstructured years of her childhood. Yet he made it sound like some particularly nasty habit.

'And how exactly do you arrive at that conclusion? I wouldn't have thought our acquaintance has been long enough to make you an authority on how I run my life!'

He laughed shortly, mockery sparkling in the depths of his eyes. 'Temper, temper! Does it annoy you so much that I find you easy to read?'

'Don't flatter yourself! You know absolutely nothing about me. If you did just happen to fall lucky and guess that I am a person who likes to plan for the future, then so what? It isn't a crime, is it?'

'Not unless it stifles you so much that you become incapable of altering those plans once they are made. Admit it, isn't that the real reason why you chose to carry on with this holiday? Because you couldn't bear to alter your arrangements and make fresh plans?'

'Of course not! Don't be ridiculous. Why should I have cancelled them anyway?'

'Why, indeed, except that I would have imagined it would be extremely painful for you to be here where you should have spent your honeymoon?'

'I . . . well, obviously I'm upset about the way things have turned out.'

'Upset? What a milk-and-water way of describing losing the man you were in love with! Or maybe you weren't in love; maybe poor old Roger had a lucky escape.'

'How dare you?' She rounded on him in fury, feeling the blood pounding sickeningly in her temples. 'Roger deserted me, remember? I am the injured party, not him!'

'Mm, so you say. But maybe Roger just finally realised that he was merely a part of your plans, and decided he wanted more from life than that.'

'No! You're wrong... quite wrong. I... I loved Roger, but there was no point in dwelling on what had happened and cancelling this holiday, even though he did his damnedest to make sure I had to.' She saw the quick look Nick gave her, and smiled sourly. 'Oh, yes, you can save your sympathy for him. He doesn't need any of it, believe me! He went ahead and tried to cancel the holiday without even having the courtesy to consult with me first. It was pure chance that I found out about it and informed the travel firm that the arrangements weren't to be altered!'

'I see. Well, at least that helps explain how the mix-up in the bookings occurred. Obviously the villa was re-let to me after Roger cancelled, then, apparently, that was somehow overlooked when you insisted on keeping to the arrangements.'

'I suppose so.' Neeve sat back in her seat, lifting the glass to her lips. Nick's accusations had hit a nerve, making her wonder if there weren't more than a grain of truth in what he'd said about her relationship with Roger. Had she really been in love with him, or had he just fitted neatly into the life she'd mapped out for herself and measured up to the requirements she sought in a husband? It was a disquieting thought, as was the fact that Nick had had such little difficulty in divining it. Was she really such an open book to him that he could look into her mind and see things she was barely aware of herself? She hoped not, because it gave him a power over her that she didn't want him to have.

Abruptly she set her glass down and pushed back her chair, anxious to put an end to the disquieting interlude.

'Running away?'

'No!' She forced her voice down an octave or two, not wanting him to see how disturbed she felt. 'Of course not. There is nothing to run away from.' She shrugged, her eyes skimming over his face, then moving hurriedly away, unable to meet the intent scrutiny. 'You're entitled to your neat little theories but, no matter how entertaining this bit of psycho-analysis has been, I'd be grateful if you'd keep your opinions to yourself in future. I may be sharing this house with you, but that doesn't give you any right to start delving into my life.'

'That's fine by me. Believe me, I have no inclination whatsoever to get caught up in your affairs. However, I do feel I have the right to point out the dangers you face by acting out of character. It's obvious that recent events have thrown you off course, but I won't always be around to pick up the pieces if you get yourself into trouble.'

'No one asked you to! And I have no idea what you mean about my acting out of character.'

He laughed grimly. 'No? Then what do you call agreeing to share the villa with a stranger? I doubt if that kind of behaviour fits your usual pattern of careful forward planning!'

'Ohhh!' Incensed that he should turn the tables on her so easily, Neeve stood up to storm back to the house, then made a grab for the wine bottle as she sent it skittering across the veranda. Her sunburned shoulder grazed against the metal arm of the sun-lounger, and she shot upright, gasping in pain.

'Are you all right?'

Nick stood up, pushing aside the soft folds of the cotton robe as he examined her shoulder. Neeve's fingers laced into the front wrap of the robe, holding it tightly across her naked body, wishing she'd had the foresight at least to put some underwear on under the flimsy covering before venturing from her room.

'I'm fine. I just banged myself on the arm of the chair.' Her voice was hoarse with tension, and he lifted his gaze to study her face.

'Sure that's all you did? You sound as though you might have given yourself a nasty bump.'

'No, really. I'm fine. It's just the sunburn making it hurt, that's all. I probably wouldn't have noticed it otherwise.'

'Still bad, is it? That's the trouble with sunburn— it always feels twice as bad at night. I expect you're burning up now, considering the state you were in.'

He slid his hand along the top of her shoulder, his long fingers tracing softly over the heated flesh in a rhythm which sent shivers racing through every nerve-ending so that Neeve felt at once suffused with heat and touched with ice. Sensations rippled through her, wild flurries of excitement like nothing she'd ever experienced before, and she gasped, feeling the blood pounding along her veins. Hurriedly she stepped back, pulling the folds of cloth around her with hands that trembled.

'Don't do that,' she muttered.

'Sorry. I didn't mean to hurt you, but you're going to have a hard job getting any sleep tonight when you're burning up to that extent.'

'I... I'll manage. You don't need to concern yourself about me. You've done quite enough already, as you were just at pains to point out!'

There was a bite to the words but she didn't care. All she was concerned about at that moment was putting as much distance and several closed doors between herself and this man who seemed to have aroused more feelings in her in three short minutes than Roger had done in three whole years! However, it seemed that her accusation had sparked a reaction in him that she was totally unprepared for.

'All right, I might have been a bit hard on you just now, but I'm not that much of a louse that I'll stand aside and let you suffer when I can do something about easing your discomfort.'

'You can?' Just for a moment she wavered, and it was the biggest mistake she could ever have made.

'I can.' He smiled suddenly, his dark eyes gleaming with a reflection of light from the living-room, his voice stroking with a velvet-toned vibrancy along her stretched nerves. 'I know just the thing for that sunburn.'

He caught her hand to lead her across the veranda, and Neeve followed him meekly, her mind awash with all the sensations he'd ignited inside her. Opening a sliding glass door, he gave her a little push as he urged her ahead of him into the room. 'This will definitely take your mind completely off that sunburn. I can almost guarantee it.'

Still in a trance, Neeve walked inside, then stopped dead, feeling her heart surge into her throat. In a fast sweep her eyes ran round the room then came to rest on the huge expanse of double bed which seemed to dominate it.

For a moment she stood transfixed, then nearly leapt six feet into the air as Nick came inside and closed the door with a decisive little click. Wide-eyed, she swung round, twisting the belt of the robe between her fingers as she willed herself to stay calm, but another furtive glance at the bed sent all her fears multiplying like rabbits.

'Right, then. I'll just get everything set up while you get ready. I bet this was one of the things you'd been looking forward to most on this holiday and, as I said, I can almost guarantee that you'll forget all about that sunburn!'

He stepped around her, heading for the bed, and Neeve felt a sudden explosion of anger rocket to her head so that for a second she was almost speechless with rage. But mercifully it was only a momentary affliction.

'How dare you? You snivelling excuse for a man! Do you really think that I'd be willing to do *that*?' She spun round, her hair flying round her shoulders

in a silken cloud, her eyes burning. 'Is this the only
way you can get yourself a woman now...by
trickery? Well, let me tell you, Nick Barclay, it will
be a cold day in hell before I——'

'Before you what?' With a startling turn of speed
he was beside her, catching her by the shoulders to
swing her round, his eyes like black ice as they bored
down into hers. 'Oh, I think I have a pretty good
idea what you meant, so why disappoint you?'

He dragged her to him, lowering his head to take
her mouth in a bruising kiss. Neeve started to
struggle, trying desperately to twist away, but his
hand tightened, forcing her even closer against the
hard, lean lines of his body. Time after time his
mouth moved over hers in that rough assault, his
tongue forcing its way between her lips to tangle
with hers in an insistent rhythm which sent un-
wanted shivers of excitement curling through her.

Feeling her helpless response, his mouth gentled
for a moment, giving her a tantalising glimpse of
just how devastating it could be if he kissed her
with passion, not with anger. Then abruptly he
pushed her away from him, sending her staggering
backwards so that she fell on to the bed.

Heart pounding, she scrambled to right herself,
pulling the robe down over her bare thighs, expecting any second to feel the rough assault of his
hands, but he made no move towards her. He just
stood and watched her, his face set, his eyes filled
with a cold contempt which brought the colour up
her cheeks. She looked away, unable to meet the

cold disgust in the scrutiny, knowing with a sickening feeling of dread that she'd made a mistake.

'Cat got your tongue now, has it? Swallowed all those nasty accusations you were so eager to throw at me before? Or have you suddenly realised that you jumped the gun a bit?' He laughed harshly, a rough sound which made her flinch. 'What a very active imagination you have. What was it conjuring up just now—nice little pictures of you and me in that bed together? Well, answer me, then! Let's hear it all.'

He caught her chin and raised her head so that she was forced to look at him.

'I . . . I . . . Let me go!' She pulled her head away, rolling over to scramble to her feet. Pushing the long strands of hair off her hot cheeks, she forced herself to meet the icy black eyes. 'If I made a mistake, then I apologise, but you have to see it from my side.' Her gaze slid to the bed then away again, locking on a point in the middle of his chest. 'What did you have in mind, bringing me in here?'

'This!' He crossed the room and flung a door on the opposite side wide open. 'Remember the jacuzzi? I'm sure it must have have featured prominently in your careful plans for Roger! However, I intended it for a far more mundane purpose. A nice long soak in that would have been just the thing to ease that sunburn!' He laughed bitterly, slamming the door on the sight of the gleaming whirlpool bath. 'Still, let that be a lesson for me. From now on, sweetheart, you're on your own. I want nothing more to do with your problems!' He

strode across the room, and held the door open with
a mocking courtesy. 'Now I think it would be better
if you leave. I'm afraid I shall have to withdraw
my offer to let you use the bath. I wouldn't like
you to get any more wrong ideas as to my
intentions.'

On leaden legs Neeve walked towards the door,
keeping her face averted as she went past him,
wondering how she was ever going to face him again
after making such a terrible mistake.

'Oh, Neeve.' His voice was softer, and she
paused, glancing back over her shoulder to where
he was standing leaning against the door-frame,
wondering if he had suddenly decided to forgive
her.

'Yes?' There was a lilt of hope in her voice which
was snuffed out the instant he spoke.

'When I do take a woman into my bed that's
exactly what she will be—a woman, not some hysterical girl who wouldn't know the first thing about
satisfying a man. So don't worry your head on that
score, honey. You don't come even bottom of my
list of rejects!'

His eyes slid over her with open mockery before
he turned away and closed the door in her face.
Neeve stumbled along the passage to her room and
flung herself down on the bed, burying her hot face
in the pillow, hearing the mocking, contemptuous
words echoing round and round in her head. Tears
pricked her eyelids but she blinked them away. She
wouldn't cry, wouldn't give him the satisfaction of
knowing how much he'd upset her. She hated him,

and wild horses wouldn't make her shed a tear because of anything he said!

Yet, strangely, as she lay tossing and turning, it wasn't how much she disliked Nick Barclay that haunted her restless sleep, but how it had felt when his lips had softened for that moment, seeming to offer a taste of heaven...

CHAPTER FIVE

THE restless night had taken its toll, the dark circles under Neeve's eyes mute testimony to how little sleep she'd had.

With a weary sigh, she turned away from the bathroom mirror and made her way back to her room to get dressed. It was already way past nine o'clock, and usually she had breakfasted by now, but she'd stayed in her room to avoid running into Nick. She would have to face him some time, of course, but not just yet, not while the memory of what had happened was still so embarrassingly fresh.

Slipping on light cotton trousers and shirt, she picked up her shoes and padded in bare feet to the living-room, then stopped dead when she found Nick sprawled in one of the chairs, a cup of black coffee in his hand. He looked up, slicing a cold glance over where she stood hovering uncertainly in the doorway, then turned away, lifting the cup to his lips to drink. And, in that instant, Neeve knew that she had to say something, no matter how much she might dislike the idea, if they were to continue sharing the villa.

'Look, Nick, about last night, and, well, what I thought you were doing; I'm sorry. I should never have jumped to such a hasty conclusion.'

70

'Why not?'

She blinked. 'What do you mean...why not? Of course I shouldn't have. It was ridiculous to think that you would do such a thing!'

'Why was it ridiculous? Because you don't think I would be physically capable, or because, as you said so succinctly last night, no woman in her right mind would want anything to do with me?'

'I never said that!' Indignation laced her voice, and she moved further into the room, glaring down at him.

'Perhaps not in so many words, but you did say that it might be the only way I could get myself a woman.' One dark brow winged upwards in cold mockery but there was nothing mocking about his expression, the flatness in the depths of his dark eyes. Had her hasty accusation wounded that stiff pride of his again? She already knew how sensitive he was about his injury, so maybe he saw her words as yet another example of how repulsive he looked to the opposite sex.

Her annoyance faded instantly, melted away by the need to reassure him. 'I never meant it that way at all. I was frightened and angry and I said the first thing that came into my head, but I never meant to imply that, well, that you aren't... attractive.'

He laughed shortly, standing up abruptly so that she was forced to take a hasty step back away from him. 'Well, thank you, Neeve. I know where to go if I need a testimony as to my eligibility. However, I'm afraid I'm not really interested in your views.

All I ask is that you try to keep out of my way for
the next week or so, then maybe this holiday won't
turn out to be the disaster it is starting to be!'

He walked out of the room, leaving her staring
after him in fury. How dared he say that, accuse
her of ruining the holiday? His behaviour had
hardly been conducive to harmony. For two pins
she would march straight out of the villa and never
come back if she didn't have the sneaking suspicion
that she'd be playing straight into his hands!

Slipping her feet into her shoes, she left the house
and marched up the dirt path to the road, and
looked round. The whole day lay before her like a
blank piece of paper waiting for her to fill it in,
but it was difficult to know what to do with all the
hours apart from the fact that she had no intention
of spending them in that man's company!

Ferma village was just a small collection of
houses plus a few shops strung alongside the road—
hardly big enough to warrant a whole day's explo-
ration, but she had to find something to do to fill
in the time before she could safely go back to the
house without having Nick accusing her of getting
in his way.

Scuffing her feet in the dust, she wandered along
the road, but it was only when she reached a wire-
fenced enclosure that the germ of an idea struck
her and a faint smile tilted her lips.

She should be able to start writing the first line
on that blank sheet in a few minutes' time, and one
long enough to keep her out of Nick's way for the
rest of the day!

                    *   *   *

Well, she was going to be out of his way all right—
certainly for the rest of the day, and, unless she
found someone to help her, possibly for the rest of
the night!

Standing up, Neeve gave the buckled front wheel
of the moped she'd hired to go sightseeing a hard
kick, cursing her bad luck. It hadn't even been her
fault. She'd been quite happily riding along when
that coach had come up too close and run her off
the road into the deep drainage-ditch. Now it was
obvious that she wasn't going anywhere on the
machine.

She scrambled out of the ditch and stared along
the empty road, but there was no sign of any traffic,
as there had been none all morning, apart from that
coach. The only thing she could do now was start
walking back to Áyios Nicólaos and hope that she
could find help along the way. Otherwise she had
no idea how long it would take her to get there.

The sun was stronger now, and she unbuttoned
the shirt a little way, unwilling to bare her skin too
much and risk another dose of sunburn. The sound
of a car engine suddenly cut through the still
mountain air, and she stopped on the grass verge,
waiting for it to reach her, praying that the driver
would stop and offer assistance. When it drew to
a halt a few yards away she raced towards it, hardly
able to believe her luck.

'What the hell are you doing here?'

Shocked into silence, she slithered to an ungainly
halt, her eyes huge as she stared at the tall, familiar
figure who climbed out. Dumbly she stood and

stared at him, then hurriedly roused herself when she saw the mounting annoyance on his face.

'I had a bit of an accident.'

'What sort of an accident? Are you hurt?'

He strode towards her, his dark eyes skimming rapidly over her body, and for some strange reason Neeve felt a shudder run through her when she felt the force of that searching gaze. Deliberately, she looked away, trying to cope with Nick's unexpected appearance, ruing a malicious fate which had sent her *him* as her rescuer! Remembering his previous comments, he was going to have a field day once he found out about this latest little escapade.

'I'm fine. Just a few bruises, that's all. Nothing much.'

'I see. And how exactly did you get those bruises?' He smiled unpleasantly, glancing along the empty road before looking back at her. 'Not to mention, of course, how you got here.'

'I hired a moped to go sightseeing.' She looked up at him defiantly, then wished she hadn't when she saw his brows draw together ominously.

'You did what?'

'You heard me,' she said shortly.

'Oh, I heard all right. I just couldn't believe that I heard correctly! How could you have been so stupid as to do such a crazy thing?'

'What's crazy about it?' Indignation stiffened her spine, and she faced him squarely. 'I wanted to go sightseeing so I hired the machine. It was a very logical thing to do!'

'Oh, very logical. Very logical indeed to go riding around all by yourself in the middle of nowhere. Just as a matter of interest, where were you going?'

'Kritsá. Perhaps you know it, that little village where the film *Christ Recrucified* was made? I was not just riding around!'

'I know it all right. In fact, I know it well enough to confidently say that you are at least twenty miles off route and heading in the wrong direction.'

'Oh.'

'Oh, indeed.' He smiled tauntingly, crossing his arms across his chest as he studied her crestfallen expression. He was wearing black jeans and a black cotton shirt with the sleeves rolled up above the elbows, and with his dark hair and the faint shadow of beard on his chin he looked strangely intimidating and almost alarmingly male.

Neeve scuffed her feet against the loose stones, avoiding looking at him, wondering why she should suddenly be so aware of him as a man first and foremost. She dealt with both sexes in her job every day of her life but never before had she been so strangely conscious of the differences between them as she was now. Nick might annoy her intensely with his hard assurance that he was right and she was wrong, but he made her feel more feminine than she had ever felt before in the whole of her life, and that worried her a lot. Last night and what had happened was still vividly fresh in her mind, and she wanted to forget it as soon as possible, but she would never be able to do that if she kept seeing him in this new light.

'So where is this moped now?'

Dragged out of her thoughts, Neeve felt the colour rush to her cheeks when she found him watching her with that intent look which seemed to lay her innermost secrets bare. The last thing she needed to add to her embarrassment was for him to get an inkling of what was in her mind! 'It's just down the road, a couple of miles back. A coach ran me into the ditch and the front wheel is completely buckled.'

'You're damned lucky that's the only thing damaged! You could have got yourself killed riding along these narrow roads! Have you any idea how many accidents occur each year on these islands to tourists who go riding around?'

'Well, I wasn't killed, was I? So there is no point in going on about it now. All I want to know is if you'll help me, otherwise I shall have to walk back to Nicólaos and get someone out here to the machine.'

'Walk?' His voice hardened into disbelief. 'Have you any idea how far it is?'

'Not really, but what else do you suggest I do?'

'You could have tried using a bit of common sense in the first place and not got yourself into yet another mess!'

'If I'm in a mess then it's your fault!'

'My fault? And how, pray, do you work that out?' His brows winged skywards, but Neeve ignored his mockery, too incensed by his attitude to opt for caution.

'Quite easily. If I hadn't been trying to keep out of your way, as you told me to this morning, then I would never have hired the moped in the first place!'

'And if you hadn't let your imagination run riot last night, then there would have been no need for me to warn you to keep away. Sorry, Neeve, but you can't go off-loading your mistakes on to me, because it won't wash.'

He was still angry about what had happened; she could hear it in the granite tone of his voice—and who could blame him? He had been trying to help her, in his own way, and she had thrown that help back in his face in the cruellest way possible. Although she had told herself that she would never apologise again she had to try to ease the situation between them.

'Nick, last night I made a mistake and I'm sorry, but you——'

He cut short the apology, his face cold and stark. 'Forget it. It's over and done with now, and that's the end of the matter. Now come along.' He turned to walk back to his car but Neeve caught his arm. It was far from over, and they both knew it.

'No, Nick, you must let me clear the——'

He shrugged her hand away. 'I'm not interested in hearing another word on the subject. The best thing you can do is let it drop, especially as it appears that I've been saddled with you yet again. Now come on.'

Saddled with her! Why, of all the boorish, miserable... Her mind raced over a few other choice adjectives as she followed him to the car. However, it was only when he swung the vehicle round a tight bend and sent her bumping against the door that she looked out of the window and frowned.

'This isn't the way to Nicólaos.'

'Well done. Give the lady one extra point for observation. It isn't.'

She ignored his sarcasm. 'Ha, ha, very funny, but I have to go back into the town and get someone out to the moped.'

'Then I'm afraid you're doomed to disappointment. I've wasted enough time today on you, and I'm not about to waste any more by turning round and going back the way I came.' He shot a glance at the heavy black-strapped watch on his wrist. 'I'll be pushed to get there as it is, thanks to you.'

'But I don't want to come with you,' she said almost desperately.

'I don't see that you have much choice in the matter.'

'You can stop and let me out. I'd rather walk!'

'Really? All that way?'

'Yes!'

'And what happens if someone else stops and offers you a lift—will you accept and possibly find yourself in a different kind of trouble? Is that the sort of chance you want to take? Because just say the word and I'll stop.'

He slowed the car, but Neeve shook her head before turning to stare mutinously out of the window.

'Decided that you're safer with me after all?' His voice was softer than before, humming with a note which brought her head round, and she looked at him, feeling heat run along her veins as she met his eyes for one brief moment which could have been eternity. Something raced between them, some emotion so swift yet so vivid that it stole her breath. Then, abruptly, he laughed, his face dropping back into the familiar lines of mockery, and the moment fled.

'Better the devil you know, after all, eh, Neeve? Still, if it makes you feel better, then let me assure you that I no more want you with me than you want to come. So I suggest that you try to make the best of it as I'm having to do.'

He turned his attention back to the road, and Neeve looked away, staring out of the window, wondering why she felt the most ridiculous urge to cry.

Apart from a few very brief moments when he had been almost civil to her, Nick had gone out of his way to be as rude and unapproachable as possible. So why should she care that he had stated quite categorically that he didn't want her with him? And why should she suddenly feel that she'd been given a rare glimpse of something precious before having it snatched away again? It didn't make any kind of sense.

The sun was hot as it beat down on her head. Neeve moved deeper into the patch of shadow cast by the stunted olive trees which surrounded the small, square-built house. A few yards away, Nick laughed out loud, the sound carrying easily to where she sat as he listened to something the other man was saying, and she sighed.

He'd said barely a word on the drive up the rough mountain roads to this tiny village, and now he'd gone one step further by managing to exclude her completely from the conversation, although, in all honesty, it couldn't have been intentional. It was just her bad luck that the family he'd come to see could speak very little English and that Nick could speak seemingly fluent Greek.

A shadow fell across her and she looked up, shading her eyes against the sun, feeling her heart leap in a strangely disturbing way as she found him standing over her.

'You're very quiet. Are you feeling all right?'

She shrugged, plucking at the coarse strands of dusty grass. 'There's not much chance of being anything else. My Greek is about as good as their English.'

Nick sighed impatiently, crouching down on his heels. 'It's not my fault that you didn't bother to learn even a few basic phrases before coming here. Typical insular British attitude, expecting everyone else to speak English.'

Neeve glared at him, opening her mouth to let him know how wrong he was, but what was the point? It wouldn't change how he felt about her even if she did tell him that she could speak fluent French, German and Spanish, plus a smattering of several other languages, though unfortunately not Greek.

Obviously annoyed by her silence, he straightened, his face set. 'Anna has gone inside to make us something to eat. Maybe that will improve your temper and stop you from sitting here sulking.' He turned to go, then stopped. 'And don't you dare

go turning your nose up at what she offers. I won't
have you insulting these people just because their
standard of living doesn't meet with your full
approval!'

Did he really think she would be so crassly in-
sensitive? She came to her feet in a rush, but he
had already moved away and gone to the car to lift
a heavy metal case out of the boot. Curiosity got
the better of her, and Neeve followed him, watching
with surprised interest when he opened the case to
reveal a very expensive and professional collection
of cameras and lenses.

Deftly he set about unpacking the case and fitting
a lens to one of the cameras before taking a reading
from the light meter and making some adjustments
to the settings.

'What are you doing?'

He barely spared her a glance as he lined the
camera up with the front of the house. 'I should
have thought that was obvious.'

Colour stung her cheeks, and she turned away,
strangely hurt that he should keep up the hostilities
in such an unrelenting way.

'Oh, for heaven's sake! Here, make yourself
useful and hold this while I set the tripod up.' With
obvious impatience he thrust the camera into her
hands then started to assemble the metal tripod with
the ease of experience. 'To answer your question,
I'm working on a series for one of the Sunday
colour supplements showing how two seemingly
different lifestyles can exist side by side.'

He stood up, nodding towards the house where
Anna was arranging thick white plates on the table.
'Anna and Stavros both worked in hotels in

Heraklion yet had no difficulty in slotting back into
their former lifestyle here in this village when they
married and started a family. Their son is another
example of how deep the roots go. Stelios is nineteen
and works in Áyios Nicólaos, surrounded by a large
group of friends of many nationalities, yet his
heritage is ingrained in him. You would never re-
cognise him as the same person when you see him
dressed first in jeans and leather jacket and then in
national costume, leading one of the local troups
of dancers. In a few years' time he too will come
back here and carry on this way of life.'

'It sounds fascinating—that two lifestyles should
blend so easily. But I hadn't realised you were here
to work. I thought you were here to recuperate from
your acc——' She bit her lip, not wanting to ruin
the unexpected truce by mentioning his injury in
any way or form. 'Having a holiday.'

'I am, and this is a holiday compared to some
of the things I've been doing recently!'

She was itching to know what he meant, but he
said no more as he busied himself taking several
shots of the house. It was obvious that he was a
professional from the way he handled the
equipment, and something started to nag at the
back of her mind. Somewhere she had heard of
Nick Barclay, but where?

'Right, that will do for now. Anna has the meal
ready. I'll take the rest of the shots I need later.'

'How long will we be staying?'

'Why? Does it matter so much?' His mouth
curled in derision. 'But of course, I should have
realised. Well, I'm very sorry if your plans for the
day have been ruined, but I'm afraid there is still

a lot to do before I leave, so you will just have to make the best of it.'

He turned and walked back towards the house, leaving Neeve to follow him, her eyes shadowed. No matter what she did Nick always thought the worst of her, and found something to criticise in even the most innocent of actions. It brought home to her with force just how much he must dislike her, and the realisation was oddly bitter.

Forcing a smile for Anna, who had laid out an appetising spread of feta cheese, bread and black olives, she sat down at the table. Picking up the small glass of raki served with the simple meal, she tossed it back, blaming it for the sudden tears which smarted her eyes. She blinked them away and looked over to where Nick was sitting chatting to Stavros, his head thrown back as he laughed at something the man was saying so that she could see the gleam of his teeth white against his tanned skin, how his hair lay in careless disarray across his forehead in a way which made her fingers itch to smooth it back into place, and a hard little lump of pain grew in the middle of her heart.

She didn't want Nick to dislike her, didn't want him to insist on thinking badly about her. But it seemed unlikely that she would ever make him change his mind now, especially after what had happened last night.

CHAPTER SIX

THE day was endless. Neeve tried her best to fill in the hours while Nick worked, but by the time evening started to fall she was desperate to get away from the small house. It would have been easier if he had tried to involve her in what he was doing, but he didn't. He completely ignored her as though she didn't exist.

Anna tried her best to make her feel welcome, but it was difficult when there was no way they could really communicate because of the language barrier. In the end Neeve went and sat by herself under the olive trees again, closing her eyes and pretending to sleep rather than keep on causing the other woman so much trouble. If Nick had wanted to impress upon her what a nuisance he considered her to be, he couldn't have found a more effective way.

At a little after five o'clock, there was a diversion in the form of Anna's son, Stelios, who roared up on his motorbike. Drawn by the noisy throb of the engine, Neeve got up and wandered over to the house, smiling when Anna drew her forward and proudly introduced her to her handsome black-haired son.

Stelios was a few years younger than Neeve but he had an easy charm and maturity which made

her like him at once. The fact that he could speak
almost perfect English, thanks to his job in the
town, was undoubtedly a help.

When he invited her to go with him to meet some
friends who were in the village to dance at a large
party being held to celebrate a recent engagement,
she agreed at once, glad to get away from the tense
atmosphere Nick was creating. They were a happy,
noisy crowd, who made her so welcome that she
forgot the time and stayed far longer than she'd
intended. It was only when one of them announced
that it was time to get ready that she glanced at her
watch and realised how late it was.

Murmuring an apology, she left, refusing Stelios's
offer to escort her back down the path to his par-
ent's house. He was lead dancer in the troupe, and
would need time himself to get changed into his
costume before he was due to perform.

It had started to rain quite heavily, the sky pitch-
black now that night had fallen with that sud-
denness which had surprised her when she'd first
arrived on Crete, and she shivered as she hurried
down the slippery path. A sudden flash of lightning
lit the sky, turning the backdrop of mountains into
a starkly beautiful contrast of purple shadows
against the sudden silvery light, and she paused for
a moment to admire the majestic beauty of the
scenery.

'Where the hell have you been?'

The angry voice brought her spinning round, her
breath catching sharply when she almost cannoned
into Nick, who had come up behind her without

her hearing him. Rain had slicked his dark hair to his skull, emphasising the strong, clean lines of his facial bones, and plastered his thin cotton shirt to his chest, giving him a strangely primitive appearance which made Neeve's heart start to thump heavily.

'I asked where you've been!'

'With Stelios. Why?'

'And did it never occur to you to tell me where you were going?'

There was a harsh note of authority in his voice, and Neeve stiffened, disliking his tone, his assumption that she should have asked his permission. 'Frankly, no! You didn't seem too interested in what I did, so why should I have bothered?' She smiled tauntingly, pushing the wet hair back from her face. The wind had risen along with the rain, whipping her hair into an untidy tangle, but her appearance was the very least of her concerns as all the anger and frustration of the whole miserable day rose up inside her. 'Don't tell me you were worried about me, Nick. My, my, what a turn-up for the book that would be—the ice man himself actually showing he has feelings!'

His face went rigid, every bone outlined in stark relief as another flash of lightning lit the mountainside. 'I'd watch my tongue if I were you. Otherwise you might just find yourself in trouble!'

She laughed harshly. 'Trouble? And what trouble would that be, Mr Barclay? Another few hours of the silent treatment that you've been dishing out

all afternoon? Oh, I think I'll take my chances,
thank you!'

She pushed past him, anger and contempt written
all over her face, and heard him curse roughly. With
a sudden speed, he caught her arm and spun her
round to face him. Rain was lashing down now,
soaking them both as it blew in heavy swirls across
the mountainside, but neither was aware of it, held
by another far stronger element which brought the
blood hotly into her veins.

'Will you indeed? But that wasn't the kind of
trouble I was thinking of.' He laughed softly, a dark
glitter in his eyes as he drew her slowly towards him
and watched her eyes widen as he pressed her
against the long, hard lines of his body.

'Nick, I...'

'What? Not so certain that you can handle
it...the trouble I can cause?'

His mockery stung, making her respond without
a shred of caution. 'There is nothing you can do
to frighten me!'

'But maybe I'm not trying to frighten you, Neeve.
Maybe that is the last thing on my mind at the
moment!'

'I don't know what you mean! Let me go, Nick!
I don't want to play any silly games. This is neither
the time nor the place for it!'

'But I'm not playing games, Neeve. Far from it.
Believe me, this is no *childish* game. It's purely for
adults!'

There was something in his voice, something which made her heart run wild in crazy abandonment, but she fought against it.

'No! Stop it, Nick! I don't know what you're trying to do, but...'

'You don't? Even after last night?' He smiled sensuously, drawing her even closer as he tilted her face up to his. 'Surely you have some idea? You weren't quite so slow last night!'

'But you said that last night was a mistake! That you hadn't intended to... to...' Her voice tailed away into silence, but he seemed untouched by her reluctance to speak the word aloud.

'To seduce you? Is that what you're trying to say, Neeve? He laughed softly, the deep sound barely carrying above the noise of the wind, the heavy beating of the raindrops on the ground, but Neeve heard every word, felt every nuance, and her heart ran wild. 'I meant what I said. I had no intention of doing that last night, but tonight... tonight is an entirely different matter altogether.' His hands slid round her, pulling her hips into closer contact with his in an intimate little gesture which made her breath catch. 'Is this what you thought would happen last night, Neeve? First a little slow lovemaking?'

His hand cupped the rounded curve of her bottom as he moved her against him in a rhythm which made the blood surge round her veins so that her legs went weak and she had to cling to him or fall.

'No! Stop it, Nick. I don't know what you think you're playing at, but stop it!' She reached back to grasp his hands and make him free her, but he just laughed again, holding her tightly as he stared down into her frantic face.

'It's funny, but I never even thought about you that way until you hurled that hurt accusation at me, but after that—well, after that I could think of little else.' He lowered his head, his breath clouding on her wet skin, touching her cheek, the very corner of her mouth, and Neeve shuddered in a helpless response she couldn't hide, then went rigid with shock when she felt his mouth touch hers.

Delicately his lips traced hers, brushing, touching, moving on before she barely had time to register what was happening to skim a line of kisses up the wet curve of her cheek, then sliding back to settle on her mouth again with an urgency which sent a shaft of fire burning through her.

'Nick!' His name was half-protest, half-entreaty, a sigh of sound which hardly had time to touch the air before it was gone, swallowed up as his mouth opened over hers and caught it. His tongue slid inside her mouth, running hotly, swiftly around the soft contours before tangling with hers in a rhythm which sent the pulsing waves of heat along her veins.

Slowly, deliberately, his hand slid up her body, the long fingers leaving an imprint of fire on her skin as they slid over the wet, clinging fabric of her shirt before gliding softly on to her breast to tease the awakening bud of her nipple until it ached and throbbed.

Overcome by the heady sensations, Neeve moaned softly, pressing herself against him in a rhythm as old as time, yet which was new, shocking and exciting to her. Time seemed to stand still, catching them both in some magical moment where nothing else existed except this kiss. Then, abruptly, Nick raised his head and pushed her away from him so that she felt his rejection like a physical loss, an ache of pain.

Her eyes flew open and she stared at him, feeling an icy chill invading her limbs as she saw the bleakness in his face.

'Nick, what is——?'

He cut her off with just one look, just one cold, blank stare which sent all the wonder and magic of the kiss crumbling into dust. Turning on his heel, he strode back down the path, leaving her staring after him with tears in her eyes. Like a sleepwalker, she stumbled after him, hugging her arms round her body, but nothing seemed able to warm the icy chill of that deliberate rejection. Nothing had ever hurt this much before—not even Roger's jilting of her, and the realisation filled her with fear.

She didn't want to feel this way about a man who thought so little of her that he could use her like that. She didn't want to feel as though a great hole had just been ripped in her heart. She wanted to hate Nick for what he had done just now, yet somehow it was far harder to do that than it should have been.

*   *   *

The fire was hot, burning her skin as she knelt in front of it to dry her hair. Twisting round, Neeve ran her fingers through her hair, winnowing the pale strands apart so that it soon fell in a silky cloud around her shoulders. Across the small room there was a sharp clatter as Nick set his glass down on the table a trifle roughly, but she ignored the sudden noise just as she'd ignored him since they'd got back to Anna's. She didn't want to look at him, didn't want to remember what he had done and how foolishly she'd responded to him. He had meant to pay her back for last night, and he'd succeeded probably way beyond his wildest dreams.

Anna bustled back into the room, her eyes curious as she glanced from one set face to the other. She said something to Nick, but he shook his head before glancing over at Neeve.

'Anna wants to know if you would like something to eat before we leave. I don't, but I'm sure she will be only too pleased to get you something if you want.'

Neeve shook her head, avoiding his eyes as she stood up. 'No, I'm fine. I just want to get back to the villa.'

She crossed the room and picked up her bag from the chair before turning back to Anna and forcing a warm smile to her stiff lips. The older woman had been kindness itself when they'd arrived back soaked to the skin, rushing around fetching towels and stoking up the fire so that they could get dry. Neeve was truly grateful to her, but now all she wanted to do was leave as soon as she could.

Frankly, the sooner this whole horrible day was over the better.

'*Ef—Efharistó, Anna,*' she said haltingly, shaking the woman's hand and hoping that she would understand her stumbling attempt to show her appreciation.

Anna returned the smile, glancing at Nick as she shook Neeve's hand and said something to him in rapid Greek. Nick laughed faintly and shook his head, his expression wry as he caught Neeve's eye, and she was intrigued to know what had been said, only she wouldn't ask him.

Hitching her bag on to her shoulder, she walked to the door and braced herself before stepping out into the wind. The rain had slackened now, but it was still hard enough to soak through her shirt as she ran to the car and climbed inside. Nick got in after her and started the engine, setting the car into gear before waving to Anna and Stavros, who were both standing in the doorway to see them off.

Neeve waved until they rounded a bend in the road and the house disappeared, leaving her and Nick alone in the darkness of the stormy night. How long would it take to get back to the villa from here? She had no idea, but however long it took would be too long.

Deliberately she turned her head and stared out of the window, but there was little she could see on the unlit road. The darkness was so intense now that she could barely make out the blur of the mountain as they eased cautiously round the treacherous bends, clinging tightly to the side of

the road away from the sheer drop. When Nick
suddenly slammed on the brakes and cursed
roughly, she shot bolt upright in alarm and peered
through the windscreen, her heart sinking when she
spotted the huge landslide of mud and rocks
blocking the road.

'Stay here while I take a look to see if there's any
way around.'

He climbed out of the car, slamming the door
quickly behind him to keep the rain out. Neeve sat
forward in her seat, watching anxiously as he
climbed up the mound of rocks, her heart turning
over when it gave way and Nick started to slither
towards the edge of the cliff. However, he managed
to right himself, and strode back to the car, his expression grim as he got back inside.

'Well, it looks as if we won't be going far tonight. The road is completely blocked, and there is
no way round it.'

'What are we going to do?' Her voice was
thready, her eyes huge, her mind still reeling from
the shock of seeing him sliding towards that drop.

'There's not much we can do apart from going
back to the village. It's going to take a good few
hours to clear the road, but that won't be possible
tonight. It will have to be done in daylight.' His
expression softened, his eyes almost gentle as he
studied her pale, strained face. 'Don't worry. You'll
be quite safe. Maybe a bit wet, but you must be
getting used to that tonight.'

Neeve looked away, not wanting him to know it
wasn't her safety she'd been concerned about. She

closed her eyes for a moment then opened them
hurriedly when a picture of him sliding towards the
edge of the cliff rose up to torment her.

'Come on, we'd better get going. There's no point
in hanging around here, and I don't like the look
of that hillside. There's still a hell of a lot of rock
up there which could come rolling down now that
the foundations have been loosened.'

He got out again and made his way round to her
side, holding the door against the blustery force of
the wind as she scrambled out. Rain blew into her
face, making her gasp as the cold drops stung her
skin, but he gave her no time to have second
thoughts, obviously concerned about the stability
of the hillside from the way he kept glancing up at
it.

Sliding his hand under her arm, he urged her
along the road back the way they had come, keeping
her close to his side as the force of the wind threatened to send her reeling sideways towards the sheer
drop. It seemed to take forever to get back to the
village, and by the time the lights came into view
Neeve was exhausted. It was only the firm support
of Nick's hand under her arm which kept her struggling on.

When Anna opened the door and saw them, their
clothes once again clinging wetly to their skin, she
could only gape in shock until she got herself in
hand. Quickly, she ushered them back inside and
fetched more towels, tutting when Nick explained
what had happened, before going to find Stavros,

who only confirmed what Nick had said: that the
road wouldn't be cleared until the next day.

Neeve sat by the fire, her clothes steaming in the
heat as she listened to the flow of their voices, and
to one in particular. Slowly her eyes moved to Nick
and lingered on his face, remembering her fear
when she'd thought he was going to slide over the
edge of the cliff.

How was it that this man, this stranger, had
become so important to her in such a short time?
She had been so angry before, yet anger had been
the last thing on her mind when she'd thought he
was going to disappear down the mountainside.
She'd had three years to get to know Roger, yet, if
she was honest, it was hard to remember what he
looked like now. His image had been replaced by
that of a man with dark hair and eyes and weariness
etched on his face. Was she really so shallow that
she could forget so easily the man she had been
planning to marry? It wasn't as if Nick was excep-
tionally handsome, although his face held a rugged
attraction and strength of character which would
draw any woman's eye. But there was something
about him which made thoughts of other men fade
into insignificance.

'Stavros is just going to alert the rest of the village
to what has happened. From what he says it's going
to cause no end of inconvenience for people tonight. The village is full of visitors who've come
for the party. Still, as long as no one was injured.'
Nick crouched down in front of her, the soft, warm
glow from the fire highlighting the darkness of his

hair yet seeming to soften the harsh lines of his face.
'How are you feeling now? A bit better now that
you're warm and dry?' He smiled gently, his eyes
very dark as they searched her pale face. 'Did it
give you a fright before? There was nothing really
to worry about, you know, Neeve. Once we got
away from the landslide area it was fairly safe.'

She looked away from the searching gaze,
twisting the wet towel between fingers which had
suddenly started to tremble, terrified to look at him
in case he could see what she was feeling.

'Neeve?' There was a hint of curiosity in his deep
voice as he reached out and lifted her face to stare
deep into her eyes, and she shuddered, staring
helplessly back at him.

'I thought you were going to fall over that cliff
when the rocks gave way!' The words came out in
a rush, the picture so vivid in her mind that she
could no longer hide the fear she'd felt, and his
fingers contracted against her chin. Just for a
moment he looked at her, his eyes full of something she couldn't pretend to understand, then abruptly he straightened and stepped away from her.

'Fortunately I didn't, so I wouldn't worry about
it any more if I were you. Now I think there is
something you should know, and frankly I have
the feeling that you won't be too happy when you
hear it.'

She drew in a quick breath, forcing the memory
of that moment when his eyes had met hers from
her head. 'Then I suggest you tell me what it is and
let's get it over and done with.'

'Anna and Stavros have offered to let us spend the night here in their house.'

'I see. Well, that is very kind of them, but I fail to see how it is a problem or why I won't be pleased.' Her face tightened as comprehension dawned. 'You surely still don't think that I would consider it beneath myself to stay here?'

'No, I don't.' He stopped suddenly, running a hand over his damp hair, and, if Neeve hadn't known the very idea was ridiculous, she would have sworn he was nervous.

'There's no easy way to say this, Neeve, so I may as well give it you straight. There are only two bedrooms in the house. Anna and Stavros will use one and you and I will have to share the other.'

It took a full minute for his words to sink home, sixty tiny seconds of complete shock, then abruptly she came out of her trance. 'No! There is no way I am sharing a bedroom with you, Nick Barclay, no way at all!'

'I don't think you have much of a choice.' He moved closer to her, shooting a quick glance over his shoulder at the other couple, who were watching them curiously. 'Look, Neeve, there is nowhere else to stay. The whole village is full of visitors who have come for the engagement party. There isn't a free room in the place. Stelios will have to go and stay at his uncle's just to accommodate us while Anna and Stavros use his room.'

'No! I don't care what you say, but no! I am not sharing a room with you. I would rather sleep in the barn first!'

Anger glinted in his eyes as he caught her arm and held her in front of him. 'Would you indeed? Well, frankly I would be only too pleased to let you but, unfortunately, Cretan hospitality would never allow for that. If you make a fuss then it will be Anna and Stavros who end up sleeping in the barn, not me, not you, so how do you feel about that?'

Neeve looked past him, forcing a smile when Anna nodded brightly at her, obviously wondering what was going on. Was he telling the truth? Would the other couple insist on sleeping outside in that rough-looking barn so that she could have a room to herself? She had the uncomfortable feeling they would.

'But surely they don't like the idea of our sharing a room! I mean, Cretan society is still very strict in its outlook, and the idea of unmarried people sharing a room is surely frowned upon?' It was a last-ditch attempt to make him see sense, to make him admit that there was no way on this earth that they should be sharing a bedroom, but it didn't have any effect.

'It is, but I'm afraid I have to admit to taking a bit of a liberty to overcome that rather large hurdle.'

'What do you mean?' Her eyes narrowed and she glared back at him. 'What have you done now?'

'Not a lot—maybe bent the truth just a trifle, that's all.'

He was smiling now, his eyes holding a secret amusement, a warmth which made her toes curl, but she forced the sensation aside, not trusting him one little inch. 'Nick Barclay, if you don't tell me right now what you've done, then I won't be held responsible for my actions!'

'Well, I just happened to mention to them that you are on your honeymoon and, quite naturally, they assumed that I was on honeymoon with you!'

Eyes huge, she stared at him, wondering if she'd heard correctly, but one glance at the laughter in those devil-dark eyes convinced her she had. Colour flared into her cheeks, and she spun round to avoid his gaze, knowing she would be lost if he caught a glimpse of her face just then.

On their honeymoon...her and Nick; the thought should have filled her with horror but, if she were truly honest, it didn't!

CHAPTER SEVEN

THE air was hazy with smoke, redolent with the spicy aromas from the huge platters of food placed down the centre of each trestle-table. All around the room there was talking and laughter, almost drowning out the music being played at the far end, and how Neeve wished she could just join in and forget about what was going to happen later. When Anna and Stavros had invited her and Nick to accompany them to the party, she had jumped at the chance, anxious not to spend more time than was necessary alone in the house with Nick. Now, however, she was wondering if she should have stayed behind because in the middle of this noisy, laughing throng she felt strangely alone and bereft.

'Are you OK? Have another glass of wine.' Nick turned away from the man he'd been talking to and picked up the large earthenware jug to fill her glass, but Neeve stopped him by putting her hand over the top of it.

'No more, thanks. I've had enough. I'm fine.'

He set the jug down again. 'Look, Neeve, I know you're none too pleased about what's happened, but there is absolutely nothing either of us can do. You must see that?'

'I know and I understand, but that doesn't mean I have to like it!'

His mouth tightened, his eyes boring coldly into her as he leaned closer. 'It seems to me you're making a fuss about nothing. Frankly, I think you should be thanking your lucky stars that we weren't left stranded on that mountainside. Then you really would have had something to complain about!'

'Well, quite *frankly*, I think I would have preferred being out there rather than facing the prospect of sharing a room with you!'

'Oh, yes?' He moved closer still so that his arm brushed against hers, the heat from his body flowing over her skin through the thin cotton shirt, his eyes holding hers so that she found it suddenly impossible to look away from the darkly mesmeric gaze. 'And what exactly is bothering you so much about sharing the room?'

'You know what!' She tried to add a bite to the words but for some reason they came out a trifle breathlessly, and she cringed, hating him to hear such a sign of weakness.

He smiled slowly, skimming a look over her face. 'You think I might try to carry on where we left off tonight?'

'*We* didn't leave off anything, Nick. It was you who walked away, remember? But don't imagine for a second that I'm going to let you use me like that again! I know what you were up to.' She laughed bitterly. 'Last night I made a mistake and I have apologised to you for it, but that wasn't enough, was it? You had to get your own back. But you've had your chance and that's it, as far as it goes. I have no intention of letting you do it again tonight!'

'Is that what you think I mean to do...make love to you as some kind of a punishment?'

'I don't know what you have in mind, and I don't care! All I'm saying is that if you have any funny ideas then forget them...fast! I won't be used by you or any man...for whatever reason!'

He straightened abruptly, his face like a mask. 'And I have no intention of being a substitute for your fiancé, either. I haven't forgotten what happened before, and, as you so rightly pointed out, that it was I who broke it up first! Why, I ask myself? Was it because you wouldn't be averse to a little romance, despite all your very loud protests to the contrary? After all, you have had this holiday planned for a long time now, so is it surprising that you would expect some degree of...how shall I say...sexual gratification?'

'No! How dare you say that?'

'Oh, I dare all right. But let me make this clear once and for all if you are thinking along those lines: I won't be used to provide a little diversion to liven up your holiday. The last thing I want right now is to get involved with you or any other woman. So if *you* had any plans, Neeve, along those lines, forget them!'

There was a cold contempt in his voice, and Neeve felt tears smart her eyes as she heard it. Abruptly she turned away, not wanting him to see how much he had upset her with his cold assessment.

Across the room, Stelios had appeared to lead his troupe of dancers on to the makeshift stage, looking almost unrecognisable in his soft brown breeches and boots teamed with a black shirt and black-fringed headband, and Neeve forced herself to concentrate on what was happening to keep her mind off what Nick had said, but it was impossible. The words kept echoing round and round in her head, closely followed by her own realisation that she had *never* seen Nick as a substitute for Roger, and the conclusion she arrived at was even worse. She had wanted Nick out on that hillside not because she'd been lonely and pining for another man, but for himself!

When the music started, she kept her eyes locked on the dancers, terrified to look at Nick in case some of the shock still lingered in her eyes. However, after a few minutes watching the intricate dance she was entranced, and joined the rest of the guests in an enthusiastic round of applause when it finished. There was a slight pause while the dancers conversed together, then Stelios came to the end of the platform, took the microphone and said something, and, to Neeve's dismay, she found everyone turning in their seats to stare at her and Nick, broad smiles on all their faces.

She glanced quickly at Nick and felt a little flurry of unease work its way down her spine when she saw the expression on his face.

'What's going on?' she muttered partly under her breath. 'Why are they all looking at us, Nick?'

He cast her a quick glance. 'Because Stelios has just informed the whole room that we are on our honeymoon.'

'No! Oh, Nick, you have to do something!'

'Like what?'

'Like...like anything! We can't just sit here letting them believe that. It's so dishonest!'

'Oh, there's not much danger of our sitting here. Stelios has just invited us on to the stage to join in with one of their dances—a special one that is always performed at Greek weddings.'

'No!' Her voice rose in horror as she turned fully in her seat to face him. 'Nick, I...I... Do something!'

'There isn't much I can do apart from standing up and declaring that it was all a lie, that we aren't married and on our honeymoon, and that would definitely put the damper on the whole evening for everyone.' He stood up, holding his hand out to her. 'Come on, Neeve. We shall just have to face this out, I'm afraid.'

Excuses raced through her mind, one after the other, yet deep down she knew she couldn't use even one of them to refuse, not when everyone was looking their way with a smiling expectancy. She stood up and reluctantly slipped her hand into Nick's, forcing a smile as he led her across the room to the sound of loud, enthusiastic applause.

Reaching the stage, she hesitated about scrambling up on to it, then gasped when Nick swung her up in his arms and lifted her on to the high platform before vaulting up beside her.

'You do not mind, Neeve, that everyone should know your secret?' Stelios took her hand in his, smiling down into her flushed face, obviously mistaking her heightened colour for embarrassment. 'A wedding is a source of great pleasure in Crete, and everyone wants to share your joy with you, you understand?

What could she say? 'No, of course not. It's very kind of you all. Thank you.'

'It is our pleasure.' He picked up the microphone again, and beckoned to the young couple whom Neeve had been introduced to earlier as the ones who were celebrating their engagement. They joined them on the stage, smiling shyly as they followed Stelio's bidding and joined hands with Nick and Neeve and the rest of the dancers.

The music started to play, slowly at first, and Neeve tried her hardest to follow the pattern the dancers were weaving with their feet as they moved across the stage. She stumbled as she missed a step, and Nick slid his arm around her waist, holding her firmly as he guided her through the intricate routine with a skill which surprised her. Gradually the music increased in tempo, the dancers moving faster and faster until she was quite breathless from trying to keep up with the line. Then suddenly they all broke apart into couples and she felt herself drawn tightly into Nick's arms.

Sensation shot through her at the feel of his body pressed against hers, and she faltered, her eyes lifting to his with shock in their depths. Just for a moment, a tiny split second which seemed to last

for eternity, he met her gaze, his eyes dark with
something impossible to define, then abruptly he
eased her away from him and spun her round.

Neeve closed her eyes, following him blindly, her
whole body throbbing, her heart aching for something she couldn't even put a name to. When the
music came to an end, she stood next to Nick,
hearing the noisy sound of the applause, yet it
wasn't loud enough to blot out the heavy, wild
pounding of her heart.

Stelios stepped forwards, picking up the microphone and smiling broadly as he said something,
and the whole audience laughed before picking up
a chant which echoed round and round the room.

Startled, Neeve looked round the room, trying
to work out what was happening before turning to
Nick to ask him to explain, and felt a *frisson* run
along her spine when she saw the expression on his
face. He turned his head and looked at her, his eyes
gleaming with laughter as he said softly, 'You can't
blame me this time, Neeve. I never planned any of
this.'

'Blame you for wh—oh!'

The question disappeared instantly as he turned
round and caught her by the shoulders to pull her
into his arms and kiss her with a thoroughness
which sent the blood racing along her veins. Helplessly, she clung to him, her lips soft and warm,
suddenly eager for the touch of his mouth as all
her senses went spinning out of control. Then slowly
he set her from him, taking her hand as he helped
her down from the stage and led her back to their

seats to much cheering from the appreciative audience.

He held the chair for her, then sat down beside her, his eyes running swiftly over her flushed face with something like satisfaction in their depths. Neeve drew in a shaky little breath, fighting to get herself under control again, but it was difficult when he was sitting so close to her that she could feel the hard brush of his thigh against her own, feel the heat from his skin, smell the tangy, heady aroma of aftershave which seemed even more noticeable now that her senses were alert to everything about him.

'Sorry about that,' he murmured quietly. 'But I thought it better to comply to the audience's request for a kiss rather than cause a scene.'

'I...well...yes, of course. I understand.' Deliberately she turned away from him, staring fixedly at the stage where the dancers were performing yet another gruelling routine. Of course Nick had been right to do that rather than make an issue out of the simple, well-meaning request, but how she wished it hadn't happened now of all times. With the anger burning inside her at the ruthless way he had treated her before on the mountainside, she could just have got through the rest of the night. Now, though, with the memory of that softly tantalising kiss still warming her lips, she wasn't quite so confident that she would handle it with her usual common sense!

*   *   *

The bed was soft, the crisp white sheets smelling faintly of lavender, but she couldn't relax. How could she when any moment now Nick was going to come walking through that door?

Rolling on to her side, Neeve forced herself to breathe slowly and deeply, but it did nothing to ease the panic she could feel building in her chest. She must be mad, totally and utterly mad to have let him talk her into this; yet what choice had she had? She could hardly have condemned Anna and Stavros to an uncomfortable night in the barn after all their kindness.

The door opened and colour flooded her face as Nick came into the room. He barely glanced at her, however, as he walked round the bed and sat down to unlace his trainers. Kicking them aside, he stood up and started to unbutton his shirt, and Neeve hurriedly closed her eyes, wishing she were anywhere, even on that mountainside, rather than here. How was it that the soft rustle of cotton as he stripped off his shirt could sound so loud, the dull, grating hum of the zip on his jeans make her whole body grow tense? She was being ridiculous; she was an adult, not a silly, hysterical schoolgirl, and if she couldn't handle this rather... well, awkward situation, then there was very little hope for her!

He tossed the sheet back, and she bit her lip to hold back the squeak of alarm, keeping her eyes firmly shut.

'What the hell is this?'

The astonishment in his voice brought her eyes open with a rush, and she felt her heightened colour intensify when her gaze collided with his naked chest. Just for a moment her eyes lingered on his lean torso before dropping lower to follow the direction of his pointing finger, and she felt her heart sink. At the time it had seemed such a good idea, but now, witnessing the expression of incredulity on his face, she wasn't so certain.

'It's a pillow,' she mumbled, avoiding his eyes.

'I can see that! But what the hell is it doing rammed down the middle of the bed? Surely it can't be there for the reasons which spring instantly to mind?'

There was open mockery in his deep voice as he picked up the plump feather pillow, and Neeve felt herself squirm with embarrassment. It looked so ridiculously melodramatic now, but at the time it had seemed such a sensible thing to do, to divide the double bed neatly in half.

'Well, Neeve, it can't have got there all by itself, so I can only assume that you put it there?'

'Yes!' His mockery stung. 'You can laugh all you like but that pillow stays where it is, Nick Barclay!'

'Oh, does it indeed? And do you really think it will achieve anything by being left there?'

'What do you mean?' There was a breathy huskiness to her voice as she sat up and faced him. 'Look, Nick, we have already been over all that!'

He raised a quizzical brow. 'That?'

'You taking advantage of the situation, as you very well know!'

'Well, even if I had been planning on taking advantage, that pillow would have made very little

difference one way or the other!' He tossed the
pillow across the room then pushed back the sheets,
his eyes filled with an icy amusement. 'Now shall
we try to act like adults and get some sleep? And
if it will make you feel any better, then you have
my solemn promise that you won't have need of
that pillow, so let that wild imagination of yours
have a rest, will you, Neeve? It seems to have been
working overtime recently—unless you are usually
prone to these melodramatic fancies!'

That stung, both the words and the way he had
said them in that coldly contemptuous way. 'What
happened before was hardly a fantasy!'

'And I have already told you that there won't be
a repeat of it, unless you are talking about that kiss
after the dance.' He skimmed a look over her
flushed face. 'That wasn't of my choosing, as you
very well know, so I suggest you forget all about
it. Believe me, your virtue couldn't be safer!'

He climbed into the bed and rolled over on his
side, presenting her with the broad, unresponsive
width of his back, and for some silly reason she
couldn't fathom Neeve felt her eyes fill with tears.
Stretching out her hand, she switched off the tiny
bedside lamp, then shifted cautiously in the bed,
careful to avoid touching him as she surreptitiously
wiped the tears away with the back of her hand.

It was ridiculous to feel hurt by what he'd said,
but she did, really hurt, as though it was the final
straw piled on the top of a whole miserable day full
of such straws.

A hiccuping sob escaped from her lips and she rammed her fist against her mouth to hold back all the others that were trying to follow it.

'What on earth is the matter now? Are you crying?'

Nick rolled over, propping himself up on his elbow as he peered through the darkness at her. He moved closer so that she could feel the warmth of his body against her back, and for some reason it made her cry all the harder.

'Neeve? What is it?' His voice was gentler than she had ever heard it, gentler than she could have imagined it would ever be, the deep tones velvety soft, and she sniffed miserably, hating herself for giving in like this.

'It can't be that bad, surely?' Reaching over, he scooped her backwards and turned her deftly so that he could look down into her face. 'Come on, tell me what's wrong.'

With infinite tenderness he ran a finger down the wet curve of her cheek to wipe away the trail of glistening tears, and Neeve felt her heart contract. This was a side of him which she had never seen before, and it threw her completely off balance.

'I'm sorry,' she whispered brokenly. 'I expect everything has suddenly caught up with me. It's silly, really.'

He sighed, pushing the hair back from her face. 'I expect it has. But you will get over it. I know it probably feels like the end of the world right now, losing the man you planned to marry, but once you get back home and start re-building your life it will all be fine. You will probably meet someone else who will come to mean just as much to you.'

What would he say if she told him that she had already met that person? He would be as shocked as she was herself to realise it. Roger had nothing to do with how she was feeling. He'd had nothing to do with it ever since she had met Nick! But there was no way she could tell him that now. It was far safer to let him go on thinking that it was Roger and the cancelled wedding she was grieving for.

'I suppose you're right.' She moved away from him, feeling instantly chilled as the warmth of his body faded from her skin. Nick Barclay wasn't for her; he had gone out of his way to impress that upon her, and she would be a fool to let herself believe otherwise. She had come on this holiday in defiance, determined to heal any wounds still festering from Roger's unexpected rejection. Now, though, she had the feeling that she might go back home with wounds so deep that it would take forever for them to heal.

CHAPTER EIGHT

NEEVE awoke with a jolt, heart racing, pulse leaping, every sense straining against the darkness. Fumbling on the bedside table for her watch, she lifted it closer as she peered at the illuminated dial. Three a.m.! What on earth had awoken her at such an hour? She'd been dreaming on and off since she'd finally managed to fall asleep, jumbled, confused dreams which made the blood rush hotly round her veins when she recalled them now, but surely they hadn't been the reason why she had woken with this feeling of panic clawing inside her?

Tossing back the sheet, she went to swing her legs out of the bed, then froze when she heard the anguished moan. She swung round, her heart almost stopping in fear when she saw Nick hunched on the side of the bed, his face contorted with pain. Scrambling off the bed, she hurried round to the other side, and fell to her knees beside him, peering into his face.

'Nick! What is it? Tell me what's wrong!'

She caught his shoulder and shook him almost roughly in her anxiety, and was rewarded by a glance from pain-dulled eyes.

'Muscle spasm.' He bit the words out, his lips stretched tightly against the force of the pain, his skin under her hand slick with sweat.

'What can I do?'

He shook his head, obviously trying to clear his
mind of the pain so that he could answer, and Neeve
felt her heart ache when she saw the stark pallor
of his face, the way that the pain had etched the
lines even deeper round his mouth.

'Massage…helps…sometimes.' The words came
out disjointed from the effort it cost him to utter
them, and he closed his eyes wearily. Neeve looked
down at his leg, seeing the way he was gripping the
long muscles in his thigh in an attempt to ease the
tortuous spasm from it.

Briskly she pushed his hands aside and replaced
them with her own, whispering a silent prayer that
she was doing the right thing. She had never given
anyone a massage before, and had no idea of the
right or wrong way to go about it, but there was
no way she could just stand there and watch him
suffering.

Hesitantly, she slid her fingers along his bare
thigh until they brushed the edge of the dark boxer
shorts he was wearing, then steeled herself to let
them slide further under the garment following the
distended muscle almost to his groin before her
nerve failed her. Back and forth her fingers worked,
kneading deeper into the flesh as she gained con-
fidence and felt some of the horrible rigidity leave
the muscles. However, it was impossible to ease it
completely while his leg was twisted awkwardly
under him.

'Do you think you can move, Nick? I need to straighten your leg out so that I can get at the back of it.'

'I'll try.'

Teeth clamped together, he tried to lift his legs round on the bed, cursing roundly when his injured one refused to obey. He fell back against the headboard, perspiration beading his forehead from the effort. Quickly, Neeve stooped down and lifted his leg into place, murmuring an apology as he moaned in pain, then knelt beside him on the bed and resumed the massage, working her fingers time after time along the hair-roughened flesh of his thigh until her shoulders ached and perspiration trickled between her breasts under the thin cotton nightdress she was wearing.

'That's enough. You'll exhaust yourself if you keep on any longer.'

His voice was still hoarse but it sounded marginally better than it had done before. Neeve stopped, her shoulders sagging wearily as she tossed the long, damp strands of hair back from her flushed face.

'I'll be all right in a minute once I get a second wind. That leg still feels cramped to me.' Unthinking, she ran her hand up over the taut muscle then felt her face flame when she realised just how intimate the gesture was. While she'd been busy trying to alleviate the pain she'd been scarcely aware of the situation, the way he was lying there dressed only in the silky dark boxer shorts. She glanced down at the nightdress Anna had lent her,

seeing for the first time how the fine cotton lawn
was sticking to her damp skin, and surreptitiously
tried to ease the delicate folds away from her breasts
before glancing back at Nick. However, it seemed
that he was unaware of anything at that moment
apart from his own discomfort, and she felt some
of her embarrassment fade.

'No, Neeve, you've done quite enough. I'll just
have to try and walk the rest of the cramp away.'

'Will that really do the trick?'

'Probably now that the worst of the attack has
eased. If I'd been at the villa I would have got in
the jacuzzi and had a good long soak because I've
found that helps tremendously, but...' he grimaced '...I haven't had an attack as bad as that
for some time now, although the doctors did warn
me it could happen if I didn't have another operation, and it appears they were right.'

His face was filled with a blend of loathing and
disgust as he stared down at his injured thigh and
the livid scar marring the brown flesh. Neeve felt
a flood of sympathy for him, realising just how hard
it must be for a man as proudly independent as he
was to be placed in such a helpless position.

'Maybe you should think about having that operation,' she said softly. 'It seems pointless to go
through this kind of pain if it can be avoided.'

He looked up, his face once more wearing its
customary blankness so that she had to physically
stop herself from reaching out and shaking him to
make him tell her what he was really thinking. Why
was it that every time she felt he was letting her get

a tiny bit closer he drew the shutters back down again and cut her out?

'We'll see. But sitting here won't achieve anything. I'd better get myself up and moving.' He swung his legs off the bed and attempted to stand up, his face going ashen when he took his weight on the leg.

Neeve scrambled off the bed and caught him, looping an arm around his waist to support him. 'Lean on me. I'll help you.'

He pulled away from her, anger burning in the depths of his eyes. 'I can manage! I'm not completely helpless, you know. You get back into bed. I shall be fine.'

There was a clipped note to the words which amounted to a dismissal, and she took immediate exception to it. Quite deliberately she moved away and walked round the bed to flick on the small bedside lamp, watching almost dispassionately when he immediately sank back down as his leg gave way again.

'Shall we see how well you can manage, then? How about walking over here and demonstrating it for me?' There was a taunting note in her cool voice which matched the smile curving her lips, and his brows lowered ominously. However, he made no comment as he placed his hands on either side to lever himself to his feet, and actually made it as far as to stand swaying perilously, although it was obvious to both of them that he would never make it across the room.

Neeve held her hand out, her voice dripping with honeyed sweetness now that she knew she was winning. He needed help, and whether he was prepared to admit it or not he was going to get it... from her! For some reason it was suddenly vital that she didn't back down now. 'Come along, then, Mr Independent; let's see you come walking all by yourself across the room... without anyone's help!'

'You are the most infuriating, irritating woman it has ever been my misfortune to meet, do you know that?' he snarled between clenched teeth, but she didn't even flinch.

'Compliments, compliments! I could listen to them for hours, but time is passing. So why not stop being childish about this, and let me help you? That way *maybe* we can both get some sleep for what is left of the night!'

It was a low jab, and she knew it had hit its mark when she saw the colour seep in a thin red line along his angular cheekbones. He said no more, accepting the arm she slid around his waist without a murmur, and leaning heavily on her for support as they walked back and forth across the small room until gradually the last of the stiffness eased.

Moving away from her, he sank down on to the bed and ran a hand over his face, which looked faintly grey in the poor light cast by the small lamp.

'Are you all right now?' she asked quietly as she stopped in front of him, disturbed by the sickly colour of his skin under the tan.

He leaned back on his hands, arching his back wearily. 'Yes. Just tired. That kind of an attack leaves me worn out, but I'll survive. Mind you, the one thing I could do with right now is a stiff Scotch!'

'I doubt if that would be on the doctor's prescription,' she said, forcing herself to adopt as light a tone as he had.

'Probably not, but by God it's just what I need right now!'

'Well, I don't know about Scotch, but how about a glass of wine? Would that help?'

'It certainly would.'

'Then give me a couple of minutes to wave my magic wand.'

She shot him a smiling glance before hurrying to the door, pausing when he said softly, 'Neeve.'

'Yes?'

'I like you better when you're playing the fairy godmother rather than the hard-hearted headmistress.'

His eyes were filled with laughter as he stared at her, and she felt her heart somersault and land somewhere in her throat. She spun round, her face fiery with colour, hearing the soft, delicious sound of his laughter echoing after her. Closing the door, she leaned weakly against the wall for a moment while she caught her breath. When he looked at her like that, his face unguarded, his eyes warm, Nick was devastating, so devastating that she would have jumped through hoops if he had asked her to, but she had to be sensible and not let herself read more into the situation than had been intended. He was just grateful to her, that was all, grateful that she had managed to help get him through that pain. She couldn't afford to let herself believe that he cared about her. To believe that would be to take the first step along a path which could only lead to heartache, and she'd had more than her share of that recently.

Somewhat sobered by the thought, she made her way quietly across the small living-room to find the jug of wine which she'd seen Anna put away earlier in the evening. It was right where she had thought it would be, and she picked it up along with a couple of the small stubby glasses sitting next to it on the shelf.

Nick was sitting propped against the headboard when she went back to the room, his long legs spread before him on top of the sheets, and Neeve faltered for an instant before making herself walk in and close the door with a hand that trembled slightly. It was so intimate to see him sitting there like that, relaxed and at ease, his bare chest gleaming a soft bronze in the lamplight. She had never been in this kind of situation before, alone in a bedroom with a half-naked man, and, no matter how she might tell herself to act like an adult, she couldn't stop the little shivers of awareness that were racing down her spine.

She took a deep breath, avoiding looking at him as she set the glasses down and started to pour the wine.

'Careful! You're spilling it everywhere. Let me do it.' Nick took the jug from her shaking fingers, filled the glasses and handed her one. Neeve took a deep swallow of the rather rough red wine, letting it slide quickly down her tight throat, praying that it would steady her nerves.

'Here. Sit down and relax. I'm sorry if what happened upset you.' He patted the bed next to him, his dark eyes warm as he studied her set face. 'I am really grateful to you for what you did just now, but come along—own up and admit that giving massages is what you do for a living. It can't have been my sheer good fortune that you have such an expert touch, even though you claim to be a fairy godmother into the bargain!'

It was hard not to laugh at such blatant teasing, and she sat down on the bed, some of the tension easing from her as he'd probably intended it to do. 'I most definitely don't!'

'Then what do you do? I have to admit that I have never shared a bed with anyone I know so little about. Have you?'

Well, she wasn't going to touch that question with a barge-pole, let alone admit that she had never shared a bed before with anyone! Colour flared in her cheeks, and she looked hurriedly down at the glass while she took a sip before replying. 'I'm a librarian, if you must know.'

'Are you indeed?' He grinned wickedly. 'Well, that's just about as far removed from a masseuse as you can get, I should think!'

'It certainly is. And after tonight I don't think I'm in any hurry to make a career change!' She looked up at him then, her face shadowed by the fear she'd felt earlier. 'I was afraid I would do something wrong before, Nick, and end up by hurting you more.'

'You did just fine. You did far more than I had a right to expect after what happened tonight. I wouldn't have blamed you if you'd just let me get on with it by myself, Neeve.'

'It doesn't matter.' She didn't want to talk about that now, didn't want to remember what had happened, how he had kissed her and how she had responded. It wasn't safe to do that now while he was sitting there looking so devastating that every bit of her that was female responded to it. Abruptly, she changed the subject, terrified that he would sense her feelings in some way. 'Are you going to have that operation when you go back home?'

His face closed, became guarded again. 'I haven't decided yet.'

'Why on earth not? It's silly to go on suffering pain like before when something can be done about it!'

'It isn't quite as straightforward as that. There are a number of risks involved—a fifty-fifty chance that my leg will be worse after the operation, making movement more limited.'

'I see. It . . . it must be difficult for you to decide what to do with those kind of options.'

'It is.' He looked down at his legs, his jaw clenched, his face set into lines of pain which she had the sudden strangest feeling had nothing to do with the injury he had suffered. Was that the key to why he acted as he did, imposed those restraints and limited how close he would let others get to him? Suddenly, she knew she had to find out, had to find the key to unlock the door to the man she sensed lay underneath.

'How did it happen, Nick? Was it some kind of an accident?' Her voice was soft, barely breaking the silence in the small room, and for a moment she wondered if he had heard her. Then, wearily, he leaned his head back against the carved wooden headboard, his eyes staring into the distance, looking back to a time and a place she knew instinctively he didn't want to remember.

'It wasn't an accident. Far from it.'

'Then how did it happen?' She held her breath, waiting, wanting him to share with her whatever it was that had hurt him so much, then almost wished she hadn't pushed him when she saw the raw agony on his face as the memories came flooding back.

'I was in Romania when it happened. It was just before the Ceausescu regime was overthrown. I'd been working on a book of photographs showing how children throughout the world are innocent victims of politics. Someone gave me a tip-off about the vast numbers abandoned in orphanages throughout Romania, although at that time it hadn't become general knowledge that the problem even existed. I went out there to see for myself if what I'd been told was right, and just happened to be in the wrong place at the wrong time, I suppose, but I don't think I shall ever forget the moment when those soldiers opened fire. It didn't matter that there were children around, that they were taking innocent lives! Those kids were the flotsam of a cruel dictator and were disposable. This leg is a memento of that day which I shall have for the rest of my life, yet I was one of the lucky ones: I lived, they didn't!'

'No! Oh, Nick, how awful for you. What can I say?'

'Nothing! There's nothing anyone can say that will wipe those memories away. I shall just have to learn to live with them.'

His voice was flat, devoid of all the emotions she could sense tearing him apart, and she wanted nothing more at that moment than to go to him and soothe them away and give him some kind of peace, yet she knew that he would reject any attempts to do that. He had made it plain that he wanted nothing from her with that deliberate rejection out on the mountainside before.

The futility of it all brought tears to her eyes, and she turned her head away, but not fast enough so that he didn't notice.

'I didn't mean to upset you.'

He was obviously concerned at what he'd thought he had done to make her cry, yet he was so completely blind to the real reason for her tears that it only made her cry all the harder. Abruptly, she stood up and made her way towards the door, desperate to get away from him before she made an even bigger fool of herself. Blinded by tears, she didn't see him get up from the bed and come towards her, so that when she walked right into him she jumped back in alarm, a tiny frightened cry issuing from her lips.

He swore softly, catching her by the waist as he held her to him, the oaths coming more freely when she started to struggle wildly.

'Stop it! What's got into you?' His hands slid up her body as he firmed his hold on her, his fingers brushing against the underside of her breasts, and she went still with shock at the sudden flare of sensations which arced between them.

'Neeve!' There was a sensual depth to his voice which flowed through her like warm, sweet wine, washing away any further thoughts of resisting. As though in a dream, she watched as he smoothed the delicate fabric of the nightdress against her breasts so that the darkened nipples were as visible to him as though she were standing there naked. Slowly, his hand moved up, his palm stroking warmly, tantalisingly, over the tautening peak in a rhythm which made a soft little moan spring from her lips.

Sensation whirled inside her, frenzied eddies of pleasure which had no beginnings, no endings, but just grew stronger with each tormenting sweep of his hand, each pleasurably painful tug of his fingers on her flesh. Then, when she thought she could stand it no longer, he drew her against him so that she could feel the hardness of his aroused body pulsing hotly against her own.

Cupping her face in his hand, he showered kisses over her face, teasing the corners of her eyes, the curl of her ear, the soft sweep of her cheek, before letting his mouth move over hers in a soft, almost gentle kiss, yet one which seemed to brand her with his mark as his lips burned against her skin.

Shaken by the wild frenzy of emotions he'd loosed inside her, Neeve locked her arms around his neck to draw him even closer so that she could feel the heavy thunder of his heart beating against her breasts, returning the kiss with a passion and abandonment which left them both breathless.

He drew back slowly, holding her eyes as he caught at the folds of the nightdress and lifted it over her head, then tossed it on to the floor in a drift of fine, pale cotton. His eyes lowered, lingering on each sweetly rounded curve as he slid his hands over the silk of her skin so that she could feel her breasts growing heavy and full, feel the tightening spiral of longing curling in the pit of her stomach.

'Beautiful, Neeve, so very beautiful that I am almost afraid to touch you in case you are a dream and you will disappear.'

His warm breath clouded on her skin just a moment before his mouth found her again, teasing her breasts in a way which sent needles of pleasure running through her. She cried out, holding his face to her, feeling the hot, smooth slide of his tongue against her flesh as her knees started to buckle. He caught her to him, his arm strong at the back of her thighs as he held her upright while he continued the tormenting caresses until she was almost mindless with longing, her body aching for the fulfilment only he could give.

When he bent and lifted her into his arms to carry her to the bed, she closed her eyes, her body throbbing with pleasure, her mind devoid of anything but the sensations he had awoken inside her. In silence he laid her down on the bed, his eyes very dark as they ran over her before he smiled gently and lay down beside her and started to trail a line of kisses down her cheek to the hollows of her throat and beyond.

Neeve sighed softly, letting the sensations sweep her away to a place of magic where nothing else existed apart from her and Nick, and the sheer wonder of what they were creating together.

CHAPTER NINE

THE sun was high in the sky, painting tiger stripes of gold and shadow across the room as it poured in through the wooden shutters.

Neeve lay in bed, her body cold as ice despite the warmth in the room, putting off the moment when she must get up and face what had happened. Maybe it would have been easier if Nick had been there beside her to offer reassurances, but he had left before the sun had risen, getting up from the rumpled bed and leaving her without a word.

She had been awake when he'd left, but she'd said nothing, made no attempt to call him back. His physical withdrawal had been a relief in a way because she had sensed his spiritual withdrawal way before that, not long after they had both come down from the dizzy, breathless heights they had climbed together.

What had happened to turn the magic of that lovemaking into ashes? Had it just been the fact that he'd discovered that she had been a virgin last night, and now regretted what had happened? She had felt the jolt of shock run through him when her body had briefly resisted his, but they had been beyond the point where they could draw back. But afterwards, he had turned away from her and lain stiff and remote, and Neeve hadn't been able to summon up the courage to make him tell her what was wrong.

Outside the house came the sound of voices, and she sat up, reaching for the sheet to wrap it around herself as she scrambled out of the bed, not wanting Nick to come back and find her lying naked in the bed. As quickly as she could she dragged on her clothes then ran a brush through the wild tangle of her hair before taking a deep breath and walking to the bedroom door. What she was going to say to Nick when she saw him she had no idea, but it had to be done. Pride demanded that she didn't remain cowering in the bedroom, no matter how awful she felt about what had happened between them.

Anna was standing at the sink washing dishes when Neeve walked hesitantly into the small living-room-cum-kitchen. She looked round and smiled, wiping her hands on her apron as she hurried across to the stove to pour her a cup of coffee. Neeve took the cup, forcing herself to smile as she took a sip of the hot liquid before glancing round the room but, mercifully, there was no sign of Nick.

Anna said something to her but Neeve had to shake her head, unable to understand a word apart from Nick's name. Where was he now? She wished she knew, wished she could extract the information from Anna so that she would have time to somehow work out what she should do, but it was impossible, thanks to the language barrier.

Tensely she went and sat down at the table, cradling the cup of hot coffee in her hands while she tried to get herself together, but when the door suddenly opened abruptly she felt all the colour drain from her face. She swung round, her heart pounding so hard that she felt physically sick, but it was only Stelios who had come into the house. He murmured a greeting to his mother, then poured himself a cup of coffee and carried it over to the table, smiling warmly at Neeve as he sat down.

'Are you wondering where Nick is? He is with the rest of the men, trying to clear the road.'

'I see. How . . . how long will it take to get it open again?'

Stelios shrugged, blowing on the hot, bitter coffee before taking a gulp of it from the cup. 'One hour...two. It's hard to say exactly. More rock had fallen than we thought. It could take longer than that, but it should be cleared before the afternoon. It's just a pity I can't stay any longer to help the others, but I have to get back to town because of my job.'

'How?' Her brow wrinkled in confusion. 'I mean, if the road is still blocked, then how can you get down into the town?'

Stelios grinned, shooting a laughing glance over his shoulder at his mother. 'Well, despite the fact that mother hates it, my motorbike is very useful! It means that I can use another path down the mountain which it would be impossible to drive down in a car.'

'Oh! I see.' She took another swallow of the bitter coffee, her mind racing as a sudden idea struck her. The last thing she wanted to do right now was face

Nick again, so surely it would be better to beg a
lift back down the mountain with Stelios. If she
could get herself back to the villa, then she would
have time to herself to think everything through and
decide what she should do. She had thought in her
innocence that she and Nick had touched the
heavens in their lovemaking, but how had he felt
about it? He had got up and left her without a
word, so maybe that said everything for him.

'Would you mind taking me with you, Stelios?
I . . . I have some things I want to do, and I really
don't want to have to waste the whole of the day
waiting around here.'

'Well, I . . .' Obviously surprised by the request,
Stelios set his cup down, a faint colour staining the
smooth, pale olive skin on his cheeks, making him
look younger than his nineteen years. 'Do you think
that is a good idea, Neeve? I mean, wouldn't Nick
be annoyed if you went off with me?'

Neeve gritted her teeth, surprised to feel tears
smarting in her eyes. 'No, of course not. Whatever
gave you that idea?'

Stelios glanced over his shoulder at his mother,
then leaned forwards across the table. 'Mother said
that Nick was angry last night when I took you to
meet my friends. I wouldn't want to start any kind
of trouble between you.'

Nick *had* been angry, but not for the reason Anna
imagined, and Neeve's heart ached afresh. The only
reason why Nick had been angry had been because
she'd had the temerity to go off without telling him

first. Nick Barclay would never be angry because
he was jealous!

She took another sip of the cooling coffee, letting
it slip down her throat, but it did little to ease the
lump of misery. She wanted to scream and shout,
to beat her fists against the wall and cry out all the
pain and anguish building inside her, but she
couldn't do that, couldn't let herself give in just
yet.

'No,' she said quietly, 'you don't need to worry
about that, Stelios. Believe me, Nick won't mind
at all if I go.'

Her bags were packed, standing neat and erect at
her feet. Neeve stared out of the window, watching
the dusty road for any sign of the taxi she'd rung
for an hour or so back. It felt like half a lifetime
since Stelios had dropped her off in Áyios Nicólaos
to catch the bus back to the villa, but it had only
been a few hours, hours which she'd spent going
back over everything that had happened before
finally coming to a decision.

Perhaps it *was* cowardly to run away, but the
thought of facing Nick again was more than she
could bear. All her life she'd held such high principles, yet where had they been last night when she
had needed them most of all? Nick had touched
her and all those principles had gone flying out of
the window. Now all she wanted was to get away
before he came back and she saw the contempt he
so obviously felt for her behaviour written all over
his face.

Abruptly, she turned away from the window and walked into the kitchen to fill the kettle with water. Her hands were shaking so much that most of the water ran down the outside of the jug but at last she managed it and plugged it in to boil. She'd had nothing to eat or drink since she'd got back to the villa, and she didn't want this now, but she made herself reach for the jar of coffee and spoon granules into a cup just to give herself something to do.

The kettle came to the boil, and she switched it off, picking it up to scald the coffee before putting it hurriedly down again when she heard a car drawing up outside. She ran back to the sitting-room to collect her cases, then froze when the door opened and Nick walked into the house.

Shock held her immobile so that for a moment all she could do was stare at him, her eyes huge, her face ashen. He met her gaze then deliberately let his eyes drop to the bags at her feet.

'Going somewhere?' His voice was cool, icily remote, like that of a stranger, not the man who had made love to her last night, and Neeve drew back as though he had struck her.

'I've decided to leave. I'm sure you will be pleased to hear it, in the circumstances.'

'And why, I wonder, should you think that?' He turned round to close the door with a slow deliberation which sent a shaft of alarm racing through her. Hurriedly she bent down and picked up the bags, using them as a shield as she moved towards

the door, but he made no attempt to get out of her
way and let her pass.

'Excuse me. I want to leave. I have a taxi due
any minute so, if you don't mind, I'll wait outside
for it.'

'Oh, but I do mind! In fact, I mind very much.'
He smiled harshly as he reached out and took the
bags from her hands to toss them across the room
so that they landed in a heap against the wall.

'How dare you? What on earth do you think
you're doing?' she rounded on him in fury. 'You
just keep your hands off my things, Nick Barclay!'

She whirled round to retrieve the cases, but she
got no further than a couple of paces before he
stopped her, his hands pinning her arms to her sides
as he glared down into her face.

'How dare I? Haven't you got that slightly
wrong? If there is anyone at fault here, then it is
you! What the hell do you think you're doing by
trying to sneak off while I was out? I couldn't believe it when I got back to Anna's and she told me
you had left. My God, Neeve, the very least you
could have done was to leave me a note, yet I doubt
you have even had the common decency to do that!'

She shook him off, anger and a bitter pain giving
her an unaccustomed strength. 'A note...saying
what? Thanks very much for last night? Sorry, but
I'm afraid my knowledge of these things is rather
limited, as you probably found out last night! I
didn't realise there was some sort of etiquette involved, but if you would like to find me a pen and
some paper then I shall be only too pleased to write

you that note!' She laughed a trifle hysterically.
'What would you like me to put? Something along
the lines of, "Dear Mr Barclay, Thank you very
much for having me, and I apologise for the fact
that I was such a great disappointment that you
found it necessary to get up in the middle of the
night and leave without a word"?'

'No! It wasn't like that at all!' He went still, his
face like a mask, the bones standing out in stark
relief as the anger drained away. He turned away
from her to run a hand over his face, and Neeve
was surprised to see how it trembled. Suddenly, with
that betraying little gesture, he became once more
Nick, the man who had come to mean so much to
her that she had willingly gone into his arms and
made love with him. If there was a chance, even a
small one, that she had been wrong to try and leave
without talking everything through with him, then
she had to be strong enough to admit it, and pride
be damned.

'Nick, last night...did it mean anything to you?'

The question hovered in the air, such a fragile
link with happiness that she wanted to reach out
and hold it, to cradle it gently in her hands, yet
there was nothing she could do but await his answer,
and pray.

He turned to face her, moving with the slowness
of a man far older, the lines of weariness etched
on his face only heightening the impression. 'Last
night was a mistake, Neeve. It should never have
happened.'

His voice was so low that it took a moment for her to comprehend what he was saying before the cold truth of it drove home.

'No! I don't believe you! You're lying to me...lying to yourself!' She pressed her hands over her ears to blot out the words, but it was impossible when they were already echoing in her head with the hollowness of a tolling bell. When he came and caught her by the arms, she fought him wildly, all thoughts of pride erased by the pain she could feel knifing through her.

'Stop it, Neeve! That won't change anything. You have to face the truth whether you want to or not!' He held her firmly, the quiet certainty in his voice draining all the fight from her so that she stopped struggling and stood limply in his grasp.

'And the truth is that it was all a mistake? Is that what you really believe, Nick?'

'Yes! You must have realised it yourself. Why else did you go running off this morning?' He glanced at the cases lying abandoned in the corner. 'Why else did you rush back here to pack your bags? Last night was a momentary madness, the result of too many passions lying dormant for too long. I *knew* how you were feeling last night, how very vulnerable you were, and I should have been strong enough to resist the physical attraction I felt for you, but I wasn't. I left you last night not because you were a disappointment but because I felt like the lowest kind of a heel for what I had done! It was a mistake, Neeve—the biggest mistake of my life, and, by God, the biggest mistake of yours!'

'How can you say that? It was more than that; you know it was! There was too much between us to just stand there and now call it some kind of a mistake, an error of judgement!'

'Then tell me what you would like to call it. Love?' He let her go abruptly, turning away to cross the room and stare out of the window, his back towards her. 'For heaven's sake, don't try to appease the guilt and embarrassment you now feel by calling it love! That's just an excuse to make it seem right in your own eyes!'

'How do you know that? I . . . I know how I felt last night, Nick.'

'Do you?' He laughed harshly. 'The same way you knew how you felt about Roger? I was just a substitute, Neeve, for the man who should have been making love to you! Why not be honest and accept it for what it was—two people who let their emotions get the better of them? Don't try to justify what you did by claiming it was love of all things!'

'Why won't you listen to me? Is it so hard to believe that I could be falling in love with you?'

'Yes, dammit, it is! You told me yourself that you always plan your life rationally, so explain how rational this is . . . falling in love with a stranger?' He turned back to her then, his eyes filled with a coldness which she felt to the very depths of her being. 'Last night was sex, Neeve, nothing more, nothing less, and no attempts to dress it up will change that!'

'What are you afraid of, Nick? Does the thought of someone falling in love with you scare you so much?'

'Yes, it does! I don't want your love, I don't want anything at all from you because I have nothing to give in return. Can't you understand that?'

'No, I can't. I can't understand why you are trying to turn last night into something sordid. What we shared was beautiful!' She drew in a shuddering breath, her eyes brimming with unshed tears, and heard him curse softly as he came back across the room to stand in front of her. Reaching out, he cupped her cheek, his fingers brushing over the soft skin in the gentlest of caresses. She closed her eyes, savouring the touch with a greedy urgency while she willed him to feel the sensations arcing between them.

Just for a second his hand lingered against her face, then slowly he let it drop to his side and Neeve opened her eyes.

'Last night you were there, Neeve, and I wanted you. That was all it was, no more, no less, and you would be foolish to let yourself think it meant more than that. Once you get back home and give yourself time to think about it, you'll realise that I'm right.'

Her face went paper-white and she recoiled from him, feeling ice sliding along her veins. Just for a second, one tiny moment out of a lifetime of empty seconds, she stared at him with despair on her face then abruptly turned away and picked up her bags from where they lay.

'Neeve, I . . .'

'No.' She didn't turn, didn't think she could ever bear to look at him again and let him see the desolation on her face. 'Don't say anything more. There's no need. You have made it all quite plain, so please let's not embarrass one another further.'

She walked towards the door, fumbling with the heavy cases as she tried to turn the handle, but he was there beside her, his hand brushing hers aside as he did it for her. Neeve fought against the desire to look at him one last time, but she was powerless to resist the urge as his hand touched hers. She turned her head and let her eyes trace over his face, memorising every line.

'Take care, Neeve. Believe me, you'll thank me for this one day.'

'Shall I? No, Nick, I don't think I shall do that.'

She walked out of the house, carrying her bags up the path just as the taxi arrived. The driver helped her with the cases then slammed the door and set off with a squeal of tyres. Neeve stared straight ahead, focusing her eyes on the road as they left the villa and Nick far behind.

CHAPTER TEN

THE library was very busy. Neeve served the next person in the long queue which stretched back from the issue desk, responding automatically to the comments the elderly lady made about a book she had just read, although her mind was far away. She'd found it increasingly difficult to concentrate since she'd got back from Crete, and now as Angela, one of the other assistants, came back from her tea-break, Neeve relinquished her place at the desk to her with a sigh of relief.

Hurriedly she made her way to the staffroom and switched on the kettle to make some coffee before dropping down into a chair and closing her eyes in despair. When would it ever end? When would this nagging sense of loss ease? It had been over a month since she'd got back, four whole weeks which she'd spent trying to convince herself that life must go on, as indeed it had, but every day was a trial and every night a fresh torment as she lay in bed remembering.

Tears filled her eyes, and she sat up and blinked them away, terrified that if she once started crying she would never be able to stop. She had told no one about what had happened on the disastrous holiday, knowing that they would never under-stand. They would have tried to cheer her up by telling her that it had all been a holiday romance, quite understandable in the circumstances, but no more than that.

She had tried to convince herself that that was all it had been, too, but in her heart she knew it was a lie. What she felt for Nick went far deeper than that, so deep that she shied away from examining how she felt too closely. There was no point, not when he had made it so plain that he felt nothing other than a fleeting sexual attraction for her. If he had left some reason to hope that things might change, then she would have snatched at it, but there was no point in deluding herself. Nick Barclay was no longer a part of her life, and she had to learn to live with that fact, no matter how hard it might be.

'Neeve, are you there?'

She jumped when Angela called her name, slopping coffee in a messy puddle on to the table. 'Yes. What's the matter? Do you need me to come back through and give you a hand?'

'No, you're OK. It's eased off a bit now, thank heavens. There's someone here to see you, though, so shall I send him through to the back?'

'Him? Who is it?'

'No idea, but if you don't want to speak to him send him back to me! Talk about tall, dark and handsome...wow!'

With a low, appreciative laugh, Angela fled back to the desk, leaving Neeve staring after her in shock. Tall, dark and handsome...she knew no one who fitted that description...apart from Nick!

She came to her feet in a rush, feeling the colour ebbing from her face as the possibility struck her. Just for a second she closed her eyes and sent up a silent prayer that she was right, then hurriedly opened them again when a man's voice said politely, 'Miss Roberts?'

He was tall, he was dark and he was, indeed, handsome, but he wasn't Nick. For a second despair showed on her face before she pulled herself together enough to respond to the question.

'Yes, I'm Neeve Roberts.'

'Well, thank heavens I've found you at last. You've led me quite a dance, I can tell you.'

There was something vaguely familiar about his voice, but she couldn't quite place what it was. For a moment she searched her memory, then felt the shock hit her afresh when she suddenly realised who he was.

'You're Nick's cousin. I spoke to you on the phone that day at the villa. Greg . . . yes, that's it— Greg Barclay.'

'Right first time. How very clever of you to make the connection so quickly.' There was open admiration in his eyes as he skimmed an assessing look over her, and Neeve felt something inside her start to ache when she saw the familiar darkness of that gaze which was so like Nick's. Deliberately she suppressed the emotion, clasping her hands tightly together to stop them from trembling in such a betraying manner.

'What do you want, Mr Barclay? How *did* you find me, in fact?'

He laughed, coming further into the room to sit down on one of the chairs so that Neeve was forced to take the one opposite rather than stand over him.

'It wasn't easy, believe me! All I had was your name to go on, seeing as Nick refused to tell us anything at all about you.' He brushed his hair back from his forehead in a gesture so reminiscent of Nick that Neeve had to look away as pain swamped her. She drew in a shaky little breath, willing herself to stay calm and see this through to the end. She had no idea why Nick's cousin had sought her out, but it couldn't be for any one of the reasons which were trying to set down hopeful roots in her heart. If Nick had wanted anything more to do with her he would have come himself.

'Yes, it really was hard going tracing you. The travel firm and the airline both refused to divulge your address even though I explained how urgent it was that I contact you. It was just sheer good luck that I found this at Nick's flat last night, and it led me here.' He pulled a paperback novel out of his jacket pocket and tossed it on to the table as he smiled rather smugly at her. 'Rather a neat bit of detective work, I think, spotting the library's address stamp on the label. It was a long shot, but it seems to have paid off, thank heavens.'

Neeve picked up the book, smoothing the shiny cover between her trembling fingers. 'I must have left it behind when I packed. I'd never even missed it before, but I still don't understand what's going on or why you're here.' She stopped, feeling the tension humming inside her so that for a moment her heart shook with it as she summoned up the strength to ask the question. 'Did Nick send you?'

Greg shook his head, the laughter fading abruptly. 'No. He has no idea at all that I've been trying to find you.'

It was just as she'd suspected, and her heart ached afresh. 'Then I fail to see what you want with me.' She stood up abruptly, clutching the book in her hands so that her knuckles showed white. 'Thank you for returning this to me. It was——'

'Nick is in hospital.'

The shock of the flat statement was so great that she felt it run through her in seismic waves, sending ripple after ripple of aftershock in its wake. She stood quite still, her whole body clenched in sudden fear so that it was difficult to make her mouth frame the question she didn't want to ask.

'Is he all right?'

Greg shrugged, his own face showing how upset he was. 'Not really.' He coughed, pulling himself together with an obvious effort. 'There is a strong chance that he won't regain full use of his leg.'

'No!' She sank down on the chair, her eyes huge, frightened as she tried to absorb the full horror of what he'd said. 'What's happened? Please, you must tell me!'

'He must have put too much strain on his leg and damaged the muscles further. He had been warned about letting it heal slowly by taking things easy, but obviously he didn't heed the warnings enough. The surgeons have been forced to operate on it again and, from what they can tell, feel that it has been a success. However, the real problem is Nick himself. He doesn't seem to *care* if he gets better or not! I know he was devastated by what happened, but I thought he'd got over that, and all the upset he had to bear with later, which didn't help. You know he was shot trying to save a group of children?'

'No.' Her voice was a bare whisper of sound, but Greg heard it and nodded.

'Yes. He ran to help them, and got into the line of fire. It was all so tragic. Most of the children were killed outright, and afterwards Nick blamed himself for not doing more, although no one could have done in the same situation. It was touch and go at first whether he would lose the leg, but he pulled through despite——' He broke off, glancing quickly at Neeve before continuing hurriedly. 'Despite several set-backs. But now all the fight seems to have left him, and he's not responding as he should be, and that, hopefully, is where you come in.'

'Me? But how can I help? Look, Greg, I have no idea what Nick has told you about us, but——'

'Nothing. Not one single, solitary word, if you want the truth; but I'm not blind. I know you and Nick must have had some sort of an argument or something, but he needs you now!'

'Needs me?' There was a bitter sadness in her voice, and she drew in a shaky breath, fighting against the tears. 'Nick doesn't need me. He doesn't need me at all, and he made that very, very plain!

We didn't quarrel, you see. How could we have when he ... he cares nothing at all about me?'

Greg reached out and took her hand. 'I think you're wrong. I don't care what that pig-headed cousin of mine has told you, but I know what he's been like since he got back home, and something is eating him, and that something is you! If you care anything at all about him, then please, please come and see him, see if you can't work whatever problem there is out, otherwise I'm afraid that Nick is never going to get better as he should.'

He stood up, feeling in his pocket for a pen to scribble an address on a piece of paper before handing it to her. 'I know you need time to think things through so I'll be staying in town overnight. If you change your mind just ring me, Neeve. It doesn't matter how late it is. I'll be there.' His face darkened in pain. 'Nick and I are very close, you see. We were brought up as brothers after his parents were killed in a plane crash, and I would do anything in my power to help him, but I can't help him now. You can, Neeve, and if you care for him as I think you do then please try to forget whatever happened between you and come to see him.'

He left the room, closing the door quietly behind him as he went. Neeve sat huddled in the chair, feeling the pain rising inside her. She wanted to run after Greg and tell him there and then that she would go with him, yet something held her back, some deep-seated fear of being hurt again. She didn't think she could bear to go to Nick and have him reject her yet again.

By closing time she could feel her head throbbing with tension, yet she was still no closer to making a decision. She locked the library then waved goodbye to Angela, aware that her friend had been giving her covert looks ever since Greg had left.

It would have been a relief to confide in her and ask her advice, yet in her heart Neeve knew that any decision she made must be hers alone.

She took her time, forgoing the bus for the chance to think things through while she walked, so that it was almost seven-thirty before she let herself into her flat. Dropping her coat and bag on a chair, she went through to the tiny kitchen and busied herself making a meal of beans on toast, then sat at the table letting it grow cold without eating a mouthful.

She didn't want to eat, didn't want to do anything apart from see Nick, yet there were no guarantees that he would want to see her. He had made his feelings very plain on that last dreadful day at the villa, so surely the sensible thing would be to stay away from him and not risk being hurt again. All her adult life she had taken the sensible route, so why was it so hard to take it now? Why should she even consider going to see him when it might only end in yet more heartache?

Because she loved him.

It was just a still, small voice echoing softly through the confusion in her head, yet growing stronger and stronger every second.

She loved him, and that love was more important to her than any amount of pride, any number of fears about being hurt herself. She loved Nick and, no matter what the outcome, she would go to him just in case it would help.

She stood up, her heart racing, her whole body trembling with a fine, tight tension as she went to the phone and dialled the number Greg had given her. He answered at the second ring as though he had been waiting for the call. Just for a moment she found it impossible to speak, overcome by a sudden attack of nerves, but he must have guessed it was her.

'Will you come, then, Neeve?'

'Yes.' Her voice was no more than a thready whisper, but she heard Greg's swift intake of breath as he heard her, then the unmistakable relief.

'Thank you. I know how much it must have cost you to agree, but thank you.'

She gave him brief instructions on how to get to her home, then replaced the receiver, leaning against the wall as the full import of what she had done hit her afresh.

What if Nick refused to see her? What if Greg was wrong and it wasn't her he needed? She knew nothing about his life, so it was possible that there was some other woman who could give him what he needed to make him fight back to full health. What if——?

Deliberately she cut off the endless flow of unanswerable questions, busying herself with packing a small case. For once in her life she was going to

have to take things step by step as they happened,
and not try to plan what was going to happen in
advance. She should be getting better at that, after
all. Ever since Nick Barclay had entered her life
she'd found all her careful attempts at planning just
a waste of time. In fact, if this carried on much
longer she was in real danger of forgetting *how* to
play things safe!

The hospital was quiet, the muted hum of noise
barely disturbing the silence in the corridors. Neeve
followed in Greg's wake along the dimly lit maze
of passages, feeling her heartbeat accelerating with
every step she took.

The whole journey had been a rush as they'd
driven at top speed along the motorways. Greg had
said little on the journey, keeping his attention
centred on his driving so that she'd been surprised
when he'd turned the car into the forecourt of the
hospital. To her mind, visiting times would be re-
stricted to daytime hours, not the middle of the
night, but Greg had been adamant that they should
try to see Nick straight away if the doctor would
allow it, and he'd been proved right. The doctor
had been only too willing to permit such an un-
orthodox visit, making Neeve realise just how concerned he must be about his patient.

Now, as they stopped outside the closed door to
the private room Nick was in, she felt her heart
leap in her throat in sudden fear for what she might
find on the other side. She put her hand out to stop

Greg from turning the handle, her eyes huge, her face ashen and bloodless in the sickly yellow light.

He smiled quickly at her, giving her cold hand a brief reassuring pat. 'It'll be all right, Neeve. Now you're here, everything is going to be fine.'

And what if it isn't? she wanted to ask. What if Nick was furious so that her visit did more harm than good? Yet she found it impossible to voice her fears aloud as she met the eyes that were so like Nick's and felt her heart twist in pain.

Reaching past him, she opened the door and walked quietly into the room, knowing she either had to do it now or not at all.

Nick was lying in bed, eyes closed, one arm raised above his head, the light from the bedside lamp spilling harshly over his pale face. He lay so still that for a moment Neeve felt herself go cold in sudden dread, but then he spoke in that granite-hard tone she remembered so well, and everything tumbled into place so that he was once more Nick, the most annoying, pig-headed and irritating man she'd ever met, and fallen in love with!

'I've already told you that I don't want any more of your damned tablets, Nurse. If I want to sleep, then I'll sleep, but I'll do it by myself, without your filthy drugs!'

'Still turning on the same old charm, I see, Mr Barclay. My, my, but the nurses on this floor must be vying with one another to attend to a real sweetie like you!'

His whole body jerked in a convulsive reaction as he heard her voice and instantly recognised it.

His eyes shot open, and he went to sit up, his face going even paler as he met some resistance from his leg, which was heavily strapped in bandages under the wire cage which protected it from the weight of the bedding. He fell back against the mound of pillows, his chest rising and falling in a frantic rhythm as he fought to get some air into his lungs, and Neeve took advantage of the moment to walk closer to the bed and smile down at him with a cloying sweetness.

'Now don't get excited. In your condition the last thing you should do, I expect, is to get excited about anything, isn't that right?'

There was a soft chuckle of laughter hastily turned into a cough as Greg followed her across the room, looking down at Nick's stunned and furious face with open amusement.

'Seems like you've met your match here, Nick. I thought I was bringing Neeve here to soothe your fevered brow, but that doesn't appear to be quite her style!'

Nick glared at him, angry colour rimming his lean cheekbones as he sliced a look to Neeve. 'I might have known you would start meddling if you got the chance. Who asked you to poke your nose in where it wasn't wanted? Dammit, Greg, I never asked you to bring her here, so you can just turn on around and take her away again!'

That hurt, the coldly cruel words cutting deep into her already wounded heart, but Neeve held back the pain. What she felt didn't matter. What did matter was that Nick looked so much more like himself now than he had looked when she'd first walked into the room. If she couldn't make him better with tenderness, then maybe she could achieve the same result with that hot anger which always seemed to spark so easily when they were together.

'Greg isn't taking me anywhere tonight, and probably not for the next couple of nights either. You need someone to take you in hand from the look of it, Nick Barclay, and I am just the person to do it!'

'Oh, and what makes you think that? Look, lady, I——'

'I believe that we've had this conversation before but, just to remind you, in case you've forgotten; the name is Neeve, or even Miss Roberts, but not *her*, not *lady*, and until you can remember that I have no intention whatsoever of standing here and listening to you a moment longer!' She swung round on her heel, ignoring Greg's murmur of protest as she brushed past him. One step, two... she was almost at the door and praying before Nick spoke, and she felt her knees go weak in relief.

'Where the hell do you think you're going? Stay here while I'm talking to you, wo——' He stopped, his voice altering subtly although it still held a hard inflexion. 'Neeve.'

It was such a small victory, so small that there was little justification for the exultation she felt when she turned back and looked at him again as he lay against the pillows, his face still flushed with anger, his dark hair mussed across his forehead.

She wanted to run to him and lay her cheek against his bare chest and tell him that she would never leave him, but she couldn't do that just yet. He had told her once that he wanted nothing from her, and that still held good until he told her otherwise.

Greg glanced from one set face to the other, then walked briskly to the door and opened it. 'There are a couple of phone calls I need to make, so I'll leave you to it. From the look of it, Neeve doesn't need me for protection; she's well able to hold her own with you, Nick! I'll be back in about ten minutes or so.'

Neeve forced a smile to her lips. 'That's fine with me. Ten minutes should be just about all I can stand of his grouchy behaviour!'

Greg laughed, shooting a quick look at his cousin. 'No comment! Just one thing, though, Neeve. Would you mind staying at my place to-night? It's a bit too late to start trying to find a hotel room now and——'

'She will stay at my flat. You have the keys, so you can take her straight there later on.'

The abruptness of the order took them both by surprise, and they turned to look at Nick, who had eased himself up against the pillows and was glaring at them with a fresh anger in his eyes, although, for the life of her, Neeve couldn't understand what had caused it. Frowning, she glanced quickly at Greg, but he just smiled complacently back, looking faintly smug.

'That's fine by me. I'll see you both in a few minutes, then. Be good, and try to remember that is an injured man you're dealing with, Neeve. Treat him gently, even though he damn well doesn't deserve it!'

He left the room, leaving a wave of silence in his wake. Neeve screwed her hands up into fists, fighting the almost overwhelming sense of panic at being left alone with Nick. She walked across the room and started to examine the cards lined up on the chest of drawers under the window, feigning an interest in the messages.

'Why did you come here?'

His voice was low, but she still jumped, sending several of the cards tumbling on to the floor. She picked them up, taking her time arranging them back into place, aware that Nick was watching her. 'Greg asked me to.'

'But why did you agree? What did you hope to gain from coming here? Nothing has changed. You have to understand that I meant everything I said that last day at the villa.'

Why was he being so deliberately cruel? From what she'd learned of him from his cousin, being cruel wasn't something Nick would usually do, yet he seemed intent on hurting her. Did he really hate her so much?

Just for a moment the thought was almost more than she could bear, and pain showed on her face.

'Neeve!' Her name sounded so sweet the way he said it in that slow, deep voice, taking her back to the other time he had said it just that way when he had held her in the bedroom then bent his head and kissed her. Memories came flooding back, hot and fierce, shockingly, vividly real, not just pale echoes of the past.

She caught her breath, her eyes meeting his across the room, and saw on his face a reflection of everything she was feeling.

Slowly, so slowly that it felt like a dream, she walked towards him and bent to lay her lips softly against the hard curve of his, feeling the quiver which coursed through his body. There was a moment when his lips softened, clung, then abruptly he turned his head away.

'I don't want you to come here any more, Neeve.'

His voice was harsh, sending a knife of pain into her heart, but she fought against it, clinging hold of those precious seconds when he had kissed her back.

'Don't you? Well, let's make a bargain, shall we, Nick? The moment you can get up out of that bed and come and tell me that you don't want me around, then I shall leave. Until then, I'm afraid you're stuck with me! I shall be a thorn in your flesh, nagging and pricking at you until you're so eager to get rid of me that you'll beg the doctors to help you walk properly again!'

His face darkened, the blood heavy under the lean, angular planes of his cheeks. 'I can have you banned from my room. I shall give the nurses instructions to keep you out of here!'

She shrugged. 'You can try if you feel like wasting your breath, but I doubt you'll succeed. From what I've heard, the nursing staff can't wait to get you

out of here, so they would let the devil himself come
into this room if it achieves that objective!'

She swung round on her heel, walking quickly to
the door, feeling pain lance through her when he
said harshly, 'Damn you, Neeve, I don't *want* you
here!'

It took everything she had, every last scrap of
strength to turn and face him with a brilliant smile
on her lips. 'Then you know what to do to get rid
of me, Nick.'

The door closed behind her and she leaned back
against the wall, letting the hot, bitter tears flow
down her face.

'Are you all right?'

Greg came up beside her, his face filled with
concern. Neeve tried to smile, wiping the tears away
with the back of her hand. 'I'll be fine. Don't worry
about me.'

'But I am worried.' He looked along the dimly
lit passage, and sighed. 'Look, Neeve, I would never
have persuaded you to come here if I'd thought
Nick was going to act like that. I've never seen him
behave in such a way before. It's completely out of
character!'

'I always did have a bad effect on his temper!'
She stood up straighter, forcing the anguish away
to be dealt with later. 'Still, maybe that can work
to our advantage. I told Nick that I had no intention of leaving until he got himself back on his
feet and came and told me to go, so maybe that
will give him the incentive to try harder!'

Greg laughed softly. 'Poor Nick mustn't know whether he's batting or bowling at present! When I think of the look on his face when he saw you...' He grinned, taking her hand in his. 'You're one heck of a woman, Neeve Roberts, and I only wish I'd had the good fortune to meet you before that irascible cousin of mine. But believe me when I say that Nick is far from indifferent to you, nor is it just anger he feels. I know him, Neeve!'

Neeve pulled her hand free. 'Maybe you do, but don't expect too much, will you, Greg? He's already threatened to have me banned from his room.' She shrugged lightly, her eyes shadowed. 'There won't be much I can do if he chooses to go ahead with it.'

'We'll see, but despite everything he said to you tonight you will stay, won't you?'

'Yes.'

'You must love him very much, Neeve?'

'Yes,' she whispered softly, glancing at the closed door. 'I love him very much.'

She led the way along the corridor, her heart aching as she wondered if there would ever come a time when she could tell that to Nick and not have him throw that love back in her face.

CHAPTER ELEVEN

NEEVE was nearly out of the shower when the phone rang. Wrapping a towel round herself, she hurried through the flat, trying to locate the insistent ringing. She'd been so tired by the time Greg had dropped her off last night that she'd done nothing more than find the spare bedroom and fall into bed. Now, as she hurried along the hall, she had a fleeting impression of pale grey walls, rich blue carpet and quiet luxury.

Opening the door to what was obviously a study, she ran to the phone and snatched it up.

'What took you so long? Surely you weren't still in bed at this time of the morning?'

Nick's voice echoed down the line, hard and tetchy, filled with irritation, yet the sweetest sound she'd heard in ages, and her knees went weak. Abruptly she sat down on a nearby leather chair, wincing as her bare thighs connected with the cool leather.

'Well, is it too much to expect an answer after all the time I've wasted waiting for you to get out of bed to answer the phone?'

'I wasn't in bed. I had just stepped out of the shower.'

'Oh.' It wasn't what he said so much as the *way* he said it in that deep, sensuous voice. Heat raced

158

along her veins and she caught her breath in a sudden gasp. It was crazy, but there was so much intimacy flowing between them at that moment that it felt as though he was there beside her, touching her, rather than miles away at the other end of a telephone connection.

Deliberately she tried to subdue the sensations, but she could hear the breathy huskiness of her tone. 'What did you want me for?'

'I...' he coughed, his voice very deep and resonant when he finally spoke. '...I was just checking that you had everything you needed.'

'Yes, thank you. Everything is fine; I'm sure Greg will help me find anything I need.' How was it possible to speak so politely, like a distant acquaintance, when her heart was hammering and her blood was racing madly?

'I'm sure he will!' There was an edge of pure steel in Nick's voice which cut through the sensuous cocoon which had enfolded her, and she started in surprise.

'Is something wrong, Nick?'

'No!' He drew in a soft breath, anger rippling along the line as he continued harshly. 'Look, if you're doing this out of some misplaced sense of pity, then forget about it. I don't need you coming here, offering sympathy or pity! I just——'

'Just hold it right there! I didn't come here to offer pity or sympathy. Frankly they would be wasted on someone like you. I came here to help and it's your hard luck if you don't like it! Now if you don't mind I would like to get dressed. I don't fancy ending up with pneumonia for my troubles.'

'I never asked you to come! As far as I'm concerned it would suit me fine if I never——'

She hung up, quite deliberately cutting the connection, knowing that she couldn't bear to hear him repeat how he didn't want her. On leaden legs she stood up and crossed the room, then stopped as the telephone rang again and kept on ringing until her head throbbed with the strident sound. She ran back and snatched it up, her heart hammering, knowing who was calling.

'And don't forget to bring me something to read when you come. At least *you* should be able to select a decent book!'

The line went dead but she held the receiver in her hand long after the dialling tone resumed. As apologies went it wasn't even worth a mention yet those abrupt words had set the first seed of hope down in her heart, and she could build her future on that fragile little link with Nick.

Buoyed up by the brief conversation, she dressed in record time, then set about exploring the flat while she waited for Greg to arrive to take her to the hospital. Set in an expensive block which overlooked the river, Nick's home was a reflection of the good taste which money could buy. Each room was furnished to perfection yet it lacked the personal little touches which turned a place to live into a real home. It was obvious from the luxury of the surroundings that he must be very successful at what he did, yet he seemed to have stamped very little of his personality on the flat. It was only when she opened the door to the huge, spacious studio that she found her first clue as to what made Nick tick.

Pushing the door further open, she walked into the room and stared with widening eyes at the rows upon rows of photographs which lined the plain white walls. Many of the photographs were mounted next to reproductions that had been made for magazines—disturbing, thought-provoking pictures of people from many countries suffering hardship, privation, war. They weren't comfortable images, but each one had a force and integrity which stopped one in one's tracks, a compassion which brought a lump to Neeve's throat. Suddenly it all came back to her, who Nick was: Nicolas Barclay, the world's top photographer of war and famine, and Nick Barclay, the man she loved, were one and the same, and her heart ached in fear as she stared once more round the room.

Had the years spent taking these photographs destroyed Nick's ability to believe in love? He had seen things which few other men had ever seen— every kind of cruelty and inhumanity, so he could have few illusions left. How could she ever hope to fight all this and make him believe that love could and did exist?

Nick was sitting up in bed, surrounded by an untidy heap of newspapers, and obviously not in the best of moods. Tossing aside a crumpled copy of the

Telegraph, he glowered at Neeve as she came into the room.

'I expected you here hours ago! What was wrong? Too busy to try and make it earlier, or suddenly changed your mind about wanting to go sick-visiting, Miss Nightingale?'

Neeve took a deep breath, still shaken by what she had discovered in the flat. 'And good morning to you, Mr Barclay. Still managing to retain that same sweet disposition, I see. Keep on like that and you'll have me thinking that you missed me, and I'm sure you wouldn't want *that* to happen!'

His face darkened with colour. 'I've missed you like a—— !'

'Thorn in the flesh?' she supplied helpfully, one light brown brow winging upwards in mockery. 'Well, miss me no more because I'm here now, and here I intend to stay for . . . oh, at least ten minutes if you're good.'

'Ten minutes? I've been waiting here for two whole hours and you have the cheek to say that you will stay ten minutes?' He pulled himself up against the pillows, his mouth thinning with anger. 'I'm surprised you bothered coming at all!'

'So am I if this is the sort of reception I get.' She glanced back at Greg, who was lounging against the door, following the heated exchange with evident amusement. 'Shall we go, Greg? You did say something about showing me around town, so why——?'

'Why don't you just get the hell out of here, Greg? You've done your bit bringing Neeve here, so as far as I can see you're no longer needed!'

Nick's voice was a low snarl as he glared at his cousin, but Greg merely smiled, seemingly unperturbed by the sudden outburst.

'It's really up to Neeve. What do you want to do, stay here or leave?'

She shrugged, feigning an indifference although her heart was aching at Nick's coldness. 'I'm not really bothered, but if Nick would prefer me to go then that's up to him. I can always come back again when, hopefully, he might be in a better temper!'

'I . . .' Nick stopped, his eyes closing, his face contracting as though he was struggling with himself in some silent inner battle. 'You may as well stay, seeing as you're here.'

Greg grinned. 'That's fine by me, as long as she is still prepared to put up with you after such graciousness.'

'Oh, I may as well, I suppose. After all, despite all that ill-temper, there isn't much that Nick can do while he's in that bed!'

It was a low shot, and she heard the angry hiss of Nick's breath as he caught the full force of it, but there was no way she was going to retract a word. If the only way to make him try to get better was by goading him, then she would do it, even though it hurt her to be so deliberately cruel.

When Greg left she walked over and sat down on a chair next to the bed, feeling her heartbeat quickening as she felt Nick watching her. Just for

a moment time seemed to contract, taking her back
to the villa when he had always seemed to watch
her in just that way. She drew in a deep breath,
fighting against the memories. All that was past
and, although it could never be forgotten, she had
to remember that the only thing that mattered now
was that Nick should get better.

'Did you manage to get some sleep after we left
last night?' Her voice was as cool as she could make
it so that she was surprised to see a dull flush of
colour run up his cheeks. He looked away, but not
before she'd seen an echo of something in his face
which made her wonder if he too had been remembering that time they had shared at the villa.
However, there was no hint of it in his voice when
he answered.

'Some. How about you? Were you comfortable
at the flat?'

'Yes, thanks. Mind you, I was so exhausted that
I just fell into bed, and don't remember a thing.
I'd only just got up when you rang this morning.'

'So I gathered.' There it was again, that same
sudden disturbing flash of intimacy which stole her
breath and made the blood pound along her veins.
Anxious to hide the effect he could have on her
with a few simple words, she hurriedly rushed on.

'What exactly have the doctors said about your
leg, Nick?'

He shrugged, his face blank as he looked past
her. 'Not much. They claim the operation has been
a success as far as they can judge at this stage, and
that with therapy I can expect to see a marked im-

provement, but they can't guarantee that it will ever
be perfect again.'

'And is that why you aren't trying...because
you're afraid that your leg won't be perfect?' She
laced her voice with scorn to hide the ache she felt
at the prognosis, seeing the flash of anger which
crossed his face to wipe away that horrible
blankness.

'It's none of your damned business!'

'Probably not, but one thing I never suspected
was that you are a coward, Nick, yet that's exactly
what you are—a coward! You're afraid to try im-
proving that leg in case it doesn't work. It's easier
to leave it like it is rather than risk any further
disappointment!'

'Coward? You above all people have the nerve
to call me that?' He leaned over and caught her
wrist to haul her towards him so that she met the
anger in his eyes from the space of inches. 'By your
own admission you've spent your life playing
everything nice and safe, making plans to avoid any
kind of upsets, and you have the gall to call *me* a
coward!' He laughed harshly, thrusting her away
from him. 'I might end up by being physically
crippled, Neeve, but you are emotionally crippled,
and that's far worse!'

'That's not true!'

'Isn't it? Then tell me one thing, just one, that
you have ever done spontaneously without weighing
up the pros and cons beforehand.'

'I slept with you!' She laughed a trifle hysterically. 'What are you saying, Nick, that I planned

that too…planned the rockfall and having to share the room?'

'Hardly. Even you couldn't manage to plan that far ahead. But that holiday was to have been your honeymoon, so maybe you just slipped a new character into a pre-ordained role, substituted me for Roger as your lover?'

'No!' She jumped to her feet, her only thought to escape from the nightmare he was creating again with his accusations. With a startling speed he caught her arm and pulled her back so sharply that she fell on to the bed, her fingers spreading across the bare warmth of his chest as she tried to steady herself.

'Does the truth hurt? Does it offend your delicate sensibilities that I know why you slept with me that night?'

'No! You're wrong. I slept with you that night because——' She stopped abruptly, the words lodged in her throat. How could she tell him why, and admit that she was in love with him? She hadn't understood it herself at the time, so how could she expect him to believe her now?

'Because you what?' His voice dropped to a husky murmur as he prompted her, which sent a shivering tingle of awareness coursing along her veins. Her eyes flew to his and, all of a sudden, in the space of a single heartbeat, the tension shifted away from anger to a raw sexuality which throbbed between them, sending her mind spinning into confusion. She licked her parched lips, feeling heat surging through her as Nick's eyes followed the movement of her tongue against her lips with a naked hunger.

'Neeve, I——'

The sound of the door opening shocked them both. Neeve jumped to her feet, her face filling with colour as she saw the speculative expression on the nurse's face as she came into the room.

'I'm sorry to interrupt you, Mr Barclay,' the woman said, glancing from one still figure to the other, 'but it's time for your physio session. Doctor said that you had agreed to go down this morning. Your visitor can wait, of course.'

Nick looked across at Neeve, and something inside her went cold when she saw the expression on his face, but not cold enough to numb her against the pain as he shook his head.

'There's no need for her to wait. We've said everything that has to be said.'

The nurse helped him from the bed, smiling apologetically at Neeve as they left the room, obviously believing that she had broken up the conversation, but Neeve knew better.

Nick didn't want her here. He had told her so many times, so why didn't she just pack her bags and leave rather than go on putting herself through all this heartache?

Because she loved him.

The answer was still the same, relentlessly, unremittingly the same as it had been before, and nothing would ever change it.

*   *   *

There was a light on in the sitting-room when she got back to the flat. It was very late; she'd spent the day since leaving the hospital walking the streets, trying to find some relief from the nagging ache in her heart. Now, as she pushed the door open and saw Greg lounging in the chair, she summoned up a smile.

'I was beginning to think you'd got lost. Nick said you left the hospital hours ago.'

She sat down on a chair, stretching her aching legs in front of her. 'I didn't feel like coming straight back here so I went for a walk. I'm sorry if you were worried about me.'

'It doesn't matter—not as long as you're all right.' He looked down at the glass he held in his hand. 'Nick been acting up again, has he?'

She sighed. 'You could say that.' She ran a hand over her ruffled hair, uncertainty etched clearly on her face. 'I still don't know if I'm doing the right thing by being here. All I seem to do is rub him up the wrong way.'

'Good!' Greg smiled when he saw her startled expression. 'Better that you do that than he sinks back into that lethargy again. The doctor had a word with me before I left the hospital tonight and told me that they have all been surprised how Nick has suddenly started making an effort again. So don't think coming here has been a waste of time, Neeve. It hasn't.'

And why was Nick suddenly making that effort? Because he wanted to get back on his feet so that he could get rid of her as soon as he could?

Tears of pain and weariness clouded her eyes, and she stood up, not wanting Greg to witness them. 'If you don't mind, I think I'll just go and run a bath. I could——'

She broke off as the telephone rang, waiting while Greg picked up the receiver, feeling the waves of despair rolling through her.

'Neeve? Yes, she's back now. She'd been for a walk to have a look round.'

Hearing her name, she glanced round, but Greg waved a hand to her to indicate that she wasn't needed as he continued, 'No, I'm afraid you can't speak to her right now, Nick. She's busy getting changed. We're going out to dinner. I thought I'd take her to that little club by the river. She's bound to enjoy it there.'

Her eyes widened, and she stared at him, but he ignored her. 'No, I've no idea what time we'll be back so don't expect her at the hospital too early, will you? We may as well take in a show first, then go on to the club afterwards and make a night of it. Still, I'll tell her you rang, Nick. Bye.'

He hung up, smiling to himself although Neeve failed to see the joke.

'And what was that all about?' she demanded indignantly.

'Just that there's more than one way to skin a cat.' He laughed at her expression of bewilderment. 'Let's just say that poor old Nick was exhibiting all the signs of jealousy just now when I told him that. I half suspected something of the sort yesterday when he nearly bit my head off after

I'd suggested that you should stay at my place, and now I'm even more certain I was right!'

She shook her head in disbelief, trying to stem the sudden heavy pounding of her heart. 'You must be mistaken. Why would Nick be jealous, unless...?' She couldn't say the words, couldn't bear to breathe life into this tiny bud of hope that was unfurling inside her.

'Unless he cares about you? He does, Neeve. Look, I don't know how much you know about Nick's background. He's usually very tight-lipped about it all, so I doubt he's told you that much, but maybe you should know a bit more than you do. It might help you understand him. I mentioned that we were brought up almost as brothers after his parents died; well, that wasn't wholly accurate. Nick spent a lot of his time in my home even before they died. He was left there each time his mother and father went off on one of their endless trips.' He sighed deeply. 'Nick's mother and mine were sisters, but they weren't a bit alike. Elaine Barclay was a shallow woman whose only aim in life was to enjoy herself with one long round of socialising. I don't think she ever wanted children, and when Nick came along she considered him to be a hindrance, and took every opportunity she could to palm him off on someone else until he was old enough to be sent to boarding-school. His father was little better—a weak man who was so totally besotted with Elaine that he agreed to anything she demanded.'

'How dreadful.' Pain darkened Neeve's eyes at the thought of how lonely Nick must have been as a child. It made her realise suddenly how fortunate she had been, yet up till then she had never appreciated the fact. Her parents had taken her everywhere with them as they had travelled around the world. Neeve had always felt faintly resentful of the fact and, once she had been old enough, had tried to put down roots and plan her life as a reaction to the crazily unstructured years of her childhood. But, no matter what, she had always known that her parents had loved her, still did love her, in fact, and they had insisted on taking her with them because they hadn't been able to stand the thought of leaving her behind.

'Obviously Nick's childhood had a great deal of bearing on how he turned out. He's always been a bit of a loner to some degree; that's why he copes so brilliantly with the kind of work he does. I had hoped he was getting it out of his system at one stage, but... There was a woman in Nick's life, you see, Neeve. I don't know much about her or what happened but, when he had the accident, from what I can gather she took one look at Nick's injuries, and the fact that he might be permanently handicapped by losing the leg, and upped and left.'

'No! How could she? I would never have——' She broke off, and Greg smiled.

'No, you wouldn't, but I think that is what Nick is afraid of. He's not had much experience of love, and what he has had from one source or another

has left him convinced that it's far easier to live
without it.'

It explained so much more about Nick, and made
the fear inside her grow stronger. How could she
ever hope to wipe out a lifetime's bitter experience?

The hospital was humming with activity as she made
her way along the corridor. All night long what
she'd learned about Nick's childhood had been
filling her head, making it impossible to rest.
Somehow she had to find a way to get past his resistance and convince him that it was worth taking
a chance again. It was so ironic, really; he had
always accused her of playing safe, yet in his own
way he was equally guilty.

Taking a deep breath, she eased the door to his
room open, then stopped short at the sight which
met her eyes. Nick was standing... actually
standing, albeit supported by a metal walking-
frame.

Joy raced through her, and she started eagerly
forwards, then froze when he spoke, obviously unaware of her as he had his back towards the door.

'If anyone is to blame, then it's you, Greg. You
should never have brought her here. Dammit, man,
can't you ever stop poking your nose into my affairs? If I had wanted to see her again then I would
have done just *that*! I don't need you running my
life and telling me what I should and shouldn't do!'
He turned awkwardly around, his bandaged leg still
stiff and obviously painful. 'I am perfectly capable
of telling Neeve what I want her to hear, and

I——' He stopped abruptly as he looked up and saw her standing frozen in the doorway, colour running in a fiery line along his cheekbones. 'Neeve! I didn't know you were there.'

She took a deep breath and then another just to prove to herself that it was possible to go on living when her heart felt as though it was breaking. What a fool she had been to ever hope to change his mind, to use her love to make him feel the same way about her. She meant nothing to him, and now was the time to finally admit it before she made an even bigger fool of herself than she had done already.

'They say listeners never hear good about themselves, and it seems they're right.' She smiled brittly, her eyes lingering briefly on Nick's shocked face before moving on, looking anywhere but at him. 'I'm glad to see that you're on your feet again. I said I wouldn't leave until you were up and able to come and tell me to go, so at least I've achieved that objective. Don't blame Greg too much. He did what he thought was right and, in a funny kind of way, it did work. Take care, Nick. Maybe I shall see you around some time.'

She turned to go, her whole body trembling, her head dizzy with the shock that was echoing along her veins.

'Wait! You can't go like this. You have to let me explain!'

'Explain what? I'm not stupid, Nick, although I admit I must have appeared to be. I don't need any explanations, thank you. I heard what you said, and that was all I needed to know.'

Tears welled into her eyes, and she spun round on her heel, terrified that she would break down and cry.

'Neeve!'

He called her name and she turned her head, her eyes meeting his across the room for one last time, than ran from the room, ignoring the angry roar of his voice as he called her back. It was over now, finally over, and there was no point in stopping to hear him couch his rejection in other terms. He had told her so many times that he didn't want her, and now she knew it to be a fact. She had taken a chance and risked her heart, and now it lay shattered around her feet.

CHAPTER TWELVE

IT WAS raining when Neeve arrived back in St
Helens, a heavy rain which soaked her jacket in
seconds and plastered her hair to her head, but she
was scarcely aware of the discomfort as she'd been
scarcely aware of anything since she'd left the
hospital.

The past few hours had passed in a daze as she'd
thrown her things together and taken a taxi to the
station to catch a train back home. Several times
while she'd been packing the phone had rung, but
she'd ignored it. The last thing she'd needed had
been apologies. They were useless, mere sops to
make Nick feel better, but they would do nothing
to help her. How could a few words ease this pain
which was tearing her apart, or mend her broken
heart?

She let herself in to the flat and dropped her bag,
standing with head bowed for several minutes as
weariness enveloped her. Her clothes were soaked,
but it wasn't until she felt the icy spasms in her
limbs that she realised how cold she was.

Stripping off the sodden jacket, she made her
way slowly to the bathroom and turned on the
shower, then took off the rest of her clothes and
stepped under the spray. The water was hot, beating
steadily against her cold skin, but it did little to

ease the numbness which seemed to have invaded
her limbs. She couldn't even seem to cry, the tears
smarting at her eyelids, knotting into a choking
lump in her throat yet refusing to flow and maybe
ease the anguish a bit. Was this what dying felt like,
this feeling of total despair, this blackness in the
soul? Without Nick to love she might as well be
dead.

She turned off the shower, stumbled unsteadily
to the bedroom, and pulled on a towelling robe
before dragging a comb through the snarled length
of her hair, then sat staring blankly at her reflection.

How was she going to go on now that she had
lost him for a second time? It had been bad enough
trying to cope last time, but how was she going to
find the strength to pick up the threads and start
weaving them into a new life for herself, one which
would never include Nick?

She never knew how long she sat there wrapped
in her misery, but it was dark when the sound of
the doorbell roused her. She glanced at the small
clock on the bedside table, surprised to see how late
it was, then stumbled to her feet, her limbs cramped
from sitting motionless for so long.

The bell rang again, and she smoothed a shaking
hand over her hair as she hurried to answer it, wondering who was calling at such an hour. She rarely
had uninvited visitors, and she didn't want one now;
the last thing she felt like doing was making small
talk.

Opening the front door, she fixed a polite smile
to her lips, ready to dismiss the visitor with a few

brief words, then felt all the colour drain from her face when she saw Nick standing outside. Seeing her sudden pallor, he murmured in concern and moved forwards, but she pushed the door to bar his way.

'Go away! I don't want to speak to you.' Her voice was shrill with the panic she could feel rolling through her in giant waves, and he swore harshly, leaning his full weight against the door to try to force it open again, but fear seemed to give her a strength she never usually possessed, and she managed to slam it shut.

'For heaven's sake, Neeve, don't be so stupid! Open this door and let me in.' He struck his fist against the wooden panels, making the whole door shake with the force of the angry blow, but it held fast.

Neeve leaned back against the wall, pressing her hands to her ears to block out the sound of his furious voice accompanied by yet more poundings on the door. She had no idea why he had come; all she knew was that there was no way she was going to let him into the flat.

He kept up the racket, pounding and shouting for a long time until she felt she would go crazy if he didn't stop. Then suddenly there was silence, and slowly she dropped her hands, her eyes wide and frightened, more alarmed by the silence than she had been by the rough curses, the demands he had made to be let in. Slowly, she crept to the door and pressed her ear to it, but she could hear nothing from the other side. Had he gone, finally realised that it was pointless standing there when she had no intention of letting him in?

The telephone rang, suddenly, shrilly, and she jumped, pressing a hand to her throat to stem the wild throbbing of her pulse. She snatched it up, her whole body trembling so much that she almost dropped the receiver and had to hold it with both hands.

'Yes?'

'Don't hang up!' Her heart turned over at the sound of his voice coming so clearly along the line, and tears misted her eyes in sudden despair.

'What do you want, Nick?' she asked brokenly. 'Why have you come here? Surely you can see that there is nothing left to say.'

'There is. There is a whole lot to say and I have no intention of leaving until you listen to me! After that, well, if you still want me to leave then I shall.'

There was a hard assurance in his voice that unleashed a wave of anger inside her. 'Well, isn't that big of you! Thank you very much, but I'm afraid that you're only wasting my time and your breath because there is nothing that you have to say that I want to hear!'

'Not even that I love you?' His voice was deep with emotion, and she went stiff with shock before slowly shaking her head, feeling the tears coursing down her face.

'No. You don't really mean that. You just feel sorry for me. But if this is your way of apologising, Nick, then I——'

'Apologising?' Anger rippled in his voice. 'Dammit, woman, I'm standing here in a cold, draughty phone-box telling you that I love you! I . . . love . . . you! Does that sound like an apology or pity?'

'I . . . I . . .' She couldn't seem to find the words, couldn't seem to control the shuddering tremor which ran through her as the blood started to flow again hotly through her veins.

His voice softened, taking on that deeply seductive note she remembered so well from that night at Anna's house. 'I love you, Neeve. I've been the biggest fool ever to let things get to this point, but please believe me. All I ask is that you let me come into the flat and explain.'

Was he telling the truth? Did he love her? She was terrified to let the idea take root and grow, terrified to feel joy in case it was taken from her again.

'I'm coming back upstairs, Neeve. Please let me in this time. We have to talk. I know it's hard, but trust me—just once more.'

He cut the connection and slowly she replaced the receiver, feeling her heart pounding sickeningly in her chest. Deep down she knew she should do something, anything, not just stand there, but it seemed impossible to move until there was a soft knock on the door. She drew in a deep breath then walked across the room and opened the door, standing back as Nick made his way with obvious difficulty into the room. Pain and weariness had etched deep grooves down each side of his mouth, making him look so vulnerable that Neeve's heart

went out to him at once, but she steeled herself
against the flood of emotions. She would listen to
what he had to say rationally, sensibly, not be
swayed by emotion.

He stared at her for a long moment, watching
the colour seeping under her pale skin, then smiled
gently as he took a couple of ungainly steps and
rested his hands on her shoulders.

'You are without doubt the most infuriating, annoying and disturbing woman I have ever met, but,
somehow, I seem to have fallen in love with you,
and all I want to know now is if you love me too.'

'But, Nick, this is——'

He bent and brushed her mouth with his, his lips
smoothing in a gentle, almost chaste caress across
the parted curve of hers before he drew back and
smiled softly into her eyes. 'No explanations, at
least not yet. Just one simple question, Neeve: do
you love me?'

A simple question yet the answer was unbearably
complex, leaving her open to so much pain if he
was lying, or so much joy if what he said was true.
It was such a risk, and she closed her eyes as she
took it, her heart almost stopping with fear.

'Yes.'

There was a moment when it felt as if the whole
world had stood still, holding its breath, waiting.
Then Nick rested his forehead against hers, and
Neeve was shocked to feel how he was shaking as
he whispered deeply, 'Thank God!'

He drew her to him then, cradling her against
him as he ran his hands unsteadily down her back

in a slow caress which set her on fire. 'I don't deserve this, sweet,' he said, his voice hoarse with raw pain. 'I don't deserve to have you love me after all I've done and the way I must have hurt you.'

'It doesn't matter. Nothing matters apart from the fact that you love me. You are sure, Nick? It isn't some kind of mistake?' Her eyes searched his, and she felt the fear leave her when she saw the love in his eyes.

'Now do you believe me?' he laughed softly, brushing a damp strand of hair back from her cheek. 'I can't believe how good it feels to tell you that at last. In fact I could stay here like this all night just telling you how much I love you if it weren't for this damned leg! It hurts my male ego to admit it, but I shall have to sit down before I fall down.'

'Of course!' She slid an arm around his waist to help him over to a chair, loving the fact that he let her help him. 'How on earth did you get here, Nick? I'm surprised that the doctors let you do such a crazy thing.'

'They didn't have a whole lot of choice, seeing as I signed myself out after I had persuaded Greg to drive me up here.'

'You did what? What a silly thing to do. Who knows what damage you could have done to your leg?' She glared at him as she eased him down into the armchair, but he just smiled, his arm tightening around her shoulders.

'No sillier than letting you go a second time. I don't want to go through anything like that ever again, Neeve. When I turned round and saw you in the doorway, saw the expression on your face——' He broke off, raw pain in his eyes as he took her hand and lifted it to his lips. 'I promise that I shall never hurt you like that again, my love.'

She smiled shakily, running a fingertip down the lean curve of his cheek. 'I hope not. It was the worst moment of my life... worse even than that day at the villa when I left. I hadn't fully realised how I felt about you then, you see. I knew I was attracted to you, but not why.' She coloured delicately but her eyes were steady as they met his. 'You seemed so convinced that I had been using you as a substitute for Roger that night, but I hadn't. It was you I wanted that night, Nick... no one else, although it wasn't until Greg came and told me that you were in hospital that I admitted to myself that I was in love with you. That's why it hurt so much to hear you blaming him for interfering by taking me to see you.'

'I know. I knew the very moment I saw the look on your face as you stood there in the doorway.' He swallowed hard. 'It made me come to my senses all at once, Neeve. Made me realise just what I was about to lose by being stubborn and refusing to admit how I felt... how I'd felt weeks ago in Crete. All along I'd tried to drive you away but, once I knew that that was it and I was never going to see you again, then I knew I couldn't let you go!'

She sank down on the floor beside his chair, resting her head against his knee, feeling the tremors of joy coursing through her at the sincerity in his

voice. 'Are you saying that you were in love with
me in Crete, Nick? That you...you loved me that
night when we stayed at Anna and Stavros's house?'

'Yes.' He ran a hand gently over her hair,
smoothing the wet strands with his fingers. 'Oh, I
tried to fight the attraction I felt for you right from
the beginning, but I couldn't seem to control it,
and that shocked me. I'd never felt that way before.
You came into my life and nearly drove me crazy
by making me want you when that was the last thing
I wanted...to get involved with anyone!' He
laughed wryly, tugging a strand of her hair in a
loving punishment. 'You have a lot to answer for,
young lady. I was determined to get my life back
together again, and along you came and knocked
everything for six!'

'But if you felt like that, why did you send me
away?' There was an echo of the pain she'd felt in
her voice, and his hand stilled.

'Because I was afraid, Neeve. Afraid to believe
that what I felt was real, afraid that somehow I'd
be hurt again.' He lifted her face up to look deep
into her eyes. 'I have a lot of hang-ups about love
which go back many years, and I shall tell you about
them one day. But suffice to say that I'd never had
any reason to believe in love. To me it was a myth,
a way to cover up sex prettily and make it into
something acceptable.' He shrugged, his expression
surprisingly free from bitterness. 'There was a
woman in my life when I had the accident. She
claimed to love me, but she couldn't handle the
thought of my being handicapped if I lost my leg.

We split up, and to me that was just another example of the myth. Then you came along and I was terrified by how I was feeling, how hurt I would be if you suddenly decided that you couldn't cope with the idea if anything went wrong, as it might very well have done.' He traced a finger softly down her cheek and across her lips. 'What I was starting to feel for you, Neeve, made me realise that I'd never been in love before. That's why I've been so rough on you the last couple of days. I was terrified that all you felt for me was pity.'

'It wasn't. I love you. I want you to get better again, but for your sake. Whatever happens, I shall never want to leave you!'

He smiled, his eyes dark with an emotion which sent a curl of heat through her. 'I'm glad to hear it, because I don't think I could let you go now.' A shadow passed over his face and his fingers tensed against her skin. 'You are quite certain how you feel, Neeve... that you are over Roger?' He looked away, a muscle beating rapidly along his jaw, mute testimony of the tension she could feel in him. 'Another reason why I sent you away was because I was afraid you were on the rebound and would regret what you had done once you came to your senses, maybe even want to try to sort things out with your fiancé. It all happened so fast on Crete that I was afraid you'd just got carried away.'

She shook her head, feeling his fingers sliding softly against her skin. 'No. I slept with you that night because I wanted you, and it was the most beautiful experience of my life. I had never realised just how two people could be so close.' She knelt and put her lips to the frantic little pulse, feeling the tension easing out of him. 'Roger means nothing to me. I don't think he ever really did. He just fitted into my plans, and I suppose he realised that and had the sense to end it before it was too late.'

'I'm glad.' He drew her closer to shower kisses over her cheeks and eyes. 'I couldn't bear to lose you now, Neeve.'

'You won't.' She laid her cheek against his chest, feeling his heart leap as she pressed herself against him. 'I love you such a lot, Nick. Thank heavens that Greg had the good sense to come and get me when you needed me.'

'I would have come to find you anyhow, but I guess you're right. For once his meddling paid off dividends.' He laughed, sliding his hands over the curves of her shoulders in a soft caress which made her shudder in longing. 'Think you can handle it, sweetheart?'

'Handle what?' Her voice was husky, and she saw the gleam in his eyes as he heard and immediately understood what had caused it. Slowly, so slowly that it was sweet agony, he trailed his fingers across the delicate outline of her collarbone. 'Handle marrying me, bad leg and all, plus my crazy cousin and the rest of his equally crazy family?'

'Is...' she swallowed down the sudden fierce surge of joy, her eyes huge and luminous '...is that a proposal?'

'Sounds very much like one to me.' He sobered
for an instant, setting her slightly away from him.
'Look, Neeve, I know I can't offer you the kind of
life you'd had worked out for yourself. My job
means that I spend a lot of time travelling the world,
and I want you with me—you must understand that
from the start! There will be no nice neat little house
and a nine-to-five job, but all sorts of strange accommodation in all sorts of countries—at least for
the time being.' He looked away as though terrified
to see her expression. 'I shall understand if you
decide that you can't cope with that kind of
existence. I know that you must have been used to
living far differently from that.'

Neeve swallowed down a chuckle of laughter.
'Oh, I think I'll survive.'

'Are you sure?' He took her hands, smoothing
the backs with his thumbs. 'I only want you to be
happy. I don't want you to come to regret marrying
me because it's not the kind of life you want for
yourself.'

She turned her hands over and raised his to her
lips, then pressed them against her cheeks in a
loving little gesture. 'There is something you should
know about me, Nick.'

He smiled, rubbing his hand against the velvety
softness of her skin. 'I know all I need to know.'

'Mm, yes, well, maybe. But let me just tell you
this one thing more.' She drew in a deep breath
then jumped straight in with her confession. 'My
parents are Glenda and Damien Roberts, and I
spent my childhood wandering the world with them,

so I shall have very little difficulty adapting to it again!'

'Glenda and Da—the painters?'

'Uh-huh...the very same. I'm not too sure where they are at the moment. Last I heard they were in Spain. I have lived in more countries than I can count, and I suppose that's what started my desire for order and stability. My childhood was spent making friends only to lose them when we moved on a few months later.'

'I can't take this in.' He shook his head, then grinned. 'You, Neeve Roberts, are full of surprises!'

'Good. I don't want you taking me for granted.'

'I shall never do that. Having very nearly lost you tonight, I shall never be that careless again. But you still haven't answered my question. Will you marry me, Neeve?'

She smiled tremulously, her heart overflowing with a joy she'd never experienced before. 'Yes.'

'Good. Now all that's to be done is to get the arrangements made and for me to get this leg sorted out.' He grimaced. 'And I suppose that means going back to the hospital and eating humble pie so that the doctors will treat me again. Still, it's worth it— there's no way I am going down the aisle with you on crutches.'

'Are you going back tonight? You said Greg had driven you here, but what have you done with him?'

'Sent him off to book himself a hotel room with strict instructions not to come back before morning.'

'Not until morning?' She frowned, a tiny spark
in the depths of her eyes as she glared at him. 'Sure
of yourself, weren't you? What if I'd sent you
packing?'

He laughed, framing her face with his strong
hands, and she felt her pulse leap at the tenderness
in his gaze. 'I took a chance that you wouldn't do
that, Neeve. You won't, will you?'

She swallowed hard, feeling the fire licking along
her veins, making her go weak with a longing only
he could assuage. 'No, but are you sure this is wise,
Nick? What about your leg? You mustn't take a
chance on damaging it any further.'

'Oh, I have no intention of doing that.'

He pulled her to him, his mouth covering hers
while he kissed her with a hunger which left her
breathless and clinging to him before he drew back
to skim a fingertip across the kiss-moist swell of
her lips. She shivered at the seductive touch, feeling
the excitement growing inside her. Slowly, his hands
slid down her arms and across the fluffy folds of
the robe to the knotted ends of the belt. 'How do
you fancy having your wicked way with me,
woman, while I am almost helpless in your
clutches?'

Neeve laughed shakily, her pulse racing so fast
that she thought she would explode as his fingers
brushed lazily against her skin. 'You forget I'm a
novice at all this. I doubt I would know where or
how to begin!'

The robe slid to the floor in a soft heap and his
hands glided tantalisingly over the soft, warm swell

of her breasts. 'Then it's about time we took steps to remedy that. We can't skimp on your education. Better to be safe than sorry, and cover every possibility.'

Neeve smiled as he drew her to him, her arms locking firmly around his neck as she pulled his head down to hers. That was a sentiment she could whole-heartedly endorse. Hadn't she always tried to play things safely... so why stop now?

PENNY JORDAN

A
COLLECTION

From the bestselling author of *Power Play*, *Silver* and *The Hidden Years* comes a special collection of three early novels, beautifully presented in one volume.

Featuring:

SHADOW MARRIAGE
MAN-HATER
PASSIONATE PROTECTION

Available from May 1992   Priced £4.99

W⬤RLDWIDE

Next Month's Romances

Each month you can choose from a world of variety in romance with Mills & Boon. Below are the new titles to look out for next month, why not ask either Mills & Boon Reader Service or your Newsagent to reserve you a copy of the titles you want to buy — just tick the titles you would like to order and either post to Reader Service or take it to any Newsagent and ask them to order your books.

Please save me the following titles:		Please tick	√
STORMFIRE	Helen Bianchin		
LAW OF ATTRACTION	Penny Jordan		
DANGEROUS SANCTUARY	Anne Mather		
ROMANTIC ENCOUNTER	Betty Neels		
A DARING PROPOSITION	Miranda Lee		
NO PROVOCATION	Sophie Weston		
LAST OF THE GREAT FRENCH LOVERS	Sarah Holland		
CAVE OF FIRE	Rebecca King		
NO MISTRESS BUT LOVE	Kate Proctor		
INTRIGUE	Margaret Mayo		
ONE LOVE FOREVER	Barbara McMahon		
DOUBLE FIRE	Mary Lyons		
STONE ANGEL	Helen Brooks		
THE ORCHARD KING	Miriam Macgregor		
LAW OF THE CIRCLE	Rosalie Ash		
THE HOUSE ON CHARTRES STREET	Rosemary Hammond		

If you would like to order these books from Mills & Boon Reader Service please send £1.70 per title to: Mills & Boon Reader Service, P.O. Box 236, Croydon, Surrey, CR9 3RU and quote your Subscriber No:..(If applicable) and complete the name and address details below. Alternatively, these books are available from many local Newsagents including W.H.Smith, J.Menzies, Martins and other paperback stockists from 6th July 1992.

Name:...

Address:...

....Post Code:............................

To Retailer: If you would like to stock M&B books please contact your regular book/magazine wholesaler for details.